SECRET BODYGUARD

B.J. DANIELS

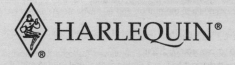

HARLEQUIN®

TORONTO • NEW YORK • LONDON
AMSTERDAM • PARIS • SYDNEY • HAMBURG
STOCKHOLM • ATHENS • TOKYO • MILAN • MADRID
PRAGUE • WARSAW • BUDAPEST • AUCKLAND

Special thanks and acknowledgment are given to
B.J. Daniels for her contribution to the
TRUEBLOOD, TEXAS series.

ISBN 0-373-22617-9

SECRET BODYGUARD

Visit us at www.eHarlequin.com

Printed in U.S.A.

ABOUT THE AUTHOR

Born in Houston, B.J. Daniels is a former Southern girl who grew up on the smell of gulf sea air and Southern cooking. But her home is now in Montana, not far from Big Sky, where she snowboards in the winters and boats in the summers with her husband and daughters. She does miss gumbo and Texas barbecue, though! Her first Harlequin Intrigue novel was nominated for the *Romantic Times Magazine* Reviewer's Choice Award for best first book and best Harlequin Intrigue. She is a member of Romance Writers of America, Heart of Montana and Bozeman Writers group. B.J. loves to hear from readers. Write to her at: P.O. Box 183, Bozeman, MT 59771.

Books by B.J. Daniels

HARLEQUIN INTRIGUE

All underlined places are fictitious.

CAST OF CHARACTERS

Amanda Crowe—All she wanted was her baby daughter back and her freedom—until she met Jesse McCall. Then she wanted it all.

Jesse Brock McCall—The undercover cop set out to catch a mobster, but the mobster's daughter had other ideas.

Susannah Crowe—The baby was missing, but had she really been kidnapped?

Gage Ferraro—Was he the grieving father he seemed to be?

J. B. Crowe—The mobster lived in a world where the only rule was to win. Even at the cost of his family?

Billy Kincaid—He left behind a legacy no one knew about.

Frank and Molly Pickett—They would have done anything for their only daughter.

Roxie Pickett—With everything she loved believed lost, she had nothing to live for.

Thomas Kincaid—The governor had his own reasons for wanting to eradicate mobster J. B. Crowe.

Mickie Ferraro—He lived by his only code of honor: greed and revenge.

Dylan Garrett—The former cop turned P.I. tried to warn Jesse what he was getting into, but Jesse wouldn't listen.

To my Aunt Eleanor,
who took me to my first scary movie
and taught me what suspense was all about,
and to my Uncle Jack, the best of the Johnsons
and my first real hero.

Chapter One

She'd sneak out tonight. He could feel it, the way he always could. A kind of static in the air. Something electric. Something both reckless and dangerous.

Jesse rubbed the cloth over the thin coat of wax on the hood of the black Lincoln town car. Reflections danced in the shine at his touch. He avoided his own reflection though, his gaze on the massive main house across the Texas tiled courtyard.

The curtains were closed in her window, but the air-conditioned breeze on the other side teased them coyly open allowing him to catch glimpses of her.

It was just like Amanda to have the window open in her wing of the air-conditioned hacienda. No wonder her scent moved restlessly through the hot, humid night. Tantalizing. Tempting. He breathed it in, holding it deep inside him as long as he could before reluctantly releasing it. Her music also drifted from her open window and hung in the thick air between the house and the chauffeur's quarters above the garage. She had the radio on the local Latin station she listened to, the music as hot and spicy as the food she liked to eat.

He rubbed his large hand over the dark, slick hood, wondering if her skin felt like this. Smooth and cool to the touch.

When she came out, it was through the side door. He stepped back into the shadows, not wanting her to see him. At first he thought she'd take the new Mercedes her father had given her for her twenty-fifth birthday, but she headed for the separate garage on the far side of the house. He watched her stick to the shadows and climb into the older model BMW parked in the first stall.

Slumming it tonight?

He waited until she'd pulled away, her taillights disappearing down the long, circuitous, tree-arched drive of the Crowe estate before he climbed on his motorcycle and followed her at a discreet distance.

Hidden cameras recorded all movement in the house and on the grounds, which meant she couldn't leave without being noticed. And yet the guard in the small stone building at the edge of the property that acted as the hub of the Crowes' all-encompassing, high-tech security system wasn't at his post as she and then Jesse breezed past.

Before she even got to the massive wrought-iron

gate that kept the rest of the world out of the sequestered compound, the gate swung open wide as if she were the princess of the palace. Which, of course, she was.

He barely slipped through behind her before the gate slammed closed, staying just close enough on his bike as she headed for Dallas, that he didn't lose her.

Night air rushed by thick and hot as he wove in and out of the traffic along the outskirts of the "Big D," keeping her in sight ahead of him, just as he had all the other nights.

Only tonight felt different. Tonight, after all his waiting, something was going to happen. He sensed it, more aware of the woman he tailed than ever before. He couldn't still the small thrill of secret pleasure that coursed through him. His heart beat a little faster.

Ahead, Amanda pulled over along a dark, nearly isolated street. He swung in behind a pickup parked at the curb and watched her get out. She glanced around as if worried she might have been followed. As if she had something to hide. He smiled to himself. Oh, she had something to hide all right.

Down the block bright red and yellow neon flashed in front of one of those late-night, out-of-the-way Tex-Mex cafés found in this part of Dallas. She walked toward it.

He waited until she was almost there before he pulled his bike back onto the street. As he cruised by, he saw her go to an outside table and sit down with a woman he'd never seen before.

At the end of the block, he turned down the alley and ditched the bike to work his way back toward the café on foot, running on adrenaline, anticipation and enough fear to know he hadn't lost his mind.

He found a spot to watch her from the shadows, close enough he could see but not hear what was being said. She was crying. He could see that, crying and talking hurriedly, nervously. He'd give anything to hear what she was saying and wondered when his heart had grown so cold, so calculating. Mostly, why he believed that Amanda Crowe was lying.

Just over twenty-four hours ago, she'd called her father to tell him that her six-month-old baby, Susannah, had been kidnapped. Her story was that she and Susannah were alone in the ladies' room of a large department store when a man burst in, knocked her out and grabbed the baby. No witnesses were in the room. Also no cops were called.

J. B. Crowe had insisted on handling the kidnapping himself and Amanda had gone along with him. In the Crowe compound, it was commonly believed that the kidnapping was part of some vendetta between Amanda's father, J. B. Crowe, and

Governor Thomas Kincaid. If you believed Kincaid capable of kidnapping. Crowe, on the other hand, was an altogether different animal, capable of anything. And, Jesse feared, so was his daughter.

Jesse watched her wipe her eyes as the waiter slid a steaming plate of food in front of her and thought about the man who'd fathered Amanda's baby. Amanda hadn't even kept him around long enough to give the baby his name. Not that Amanda needed a husband. She was a Crowe. She'd never want for anything. Nor would Susannah, for that matter, if she was ever found.

The other woman was talking now, squeezing Amanda's arm, intent, leaning in so no one could hear even though there were few diners and no one at a nearby table.

Jesse wasn't sure why or what exactly he didn't believe. That Susannah Crowe had been kidnapped? Or that Amanda really was the grieving mother she appeared to be? Something just didn't sit right. His gaze narrowed as he watched her. Amanda Crowe was lying. He'd stake his life on it. He smiled at that; he'd already risked more than his life just being here tonight.

She picked nervously at her food but the tears had stopped, her iron-clad control back, a steeliness in her that she shared with her father. Part determination. Part ruthlessness.

A baby began to cry. Amanda turned abruptly, almost spilling her water. A Mexican woman carrying an infant sat down two tables over from Amanda, pulled the baby from its carrier and rocked it, trying to still the shrill cry. Amanda turned back to her food, apparently mesmerized by what was on her plate.

A new thought struck him like a fist. Was it possible?

The waiter brought out an order to go for the woman with the baby. Amanda motioned for her check.

His pulse began to pound. The woman with the baby busily strapped the infant back into its carrier. He was too far away to see the baby's face.

Amanda didn't wait for her check. She got to her feet, tossed a bill on the table, hugged her dinner companion and rushed off toward her car.

But Jesse didn't follow her. The woman with the baby started to leave as well. His mind roiled. What he was thinking didn't make any sense, but with the Crowes, anything was possible.

He moved toward the café, not letting the woman with the baby out of his sight.

It was just some woman and her baby. No kidnapper in her right mind would bring the Crowe baby to a public restaurant. And wouldn't Amanda have raced over to the table if she thought there was even a chance that the baby might be hers?

Unless the woman wasn't the kidnapper. Unless Amanda Crowe had had her own baby abducted. But what kind of sense did that make?

The woman with the baby was leaving. He wove his way through the tables, his heart racing, as he hurried to cut her off.

She looked up, startled and a little frightened to see him. He glanced into the baby carrier, ready to grab both the woman and the child.

The baby was brown skinned, with a thick head of black hair and a pair of eyes to match. While close to the same age, the little boy looked nothing like Susannah Crowe.

He stumbled back, mumbling, "Sorry," to the startled mother as she hugged the baby protectively to her. Whatever had made him think the infant would be Susannah? Because he was convinced Amanda had done something with her baby. Made it look like a kidnapping. But why?

Feeling foolish, he moved on through the café and out the back door to the alley. Amanda was gone. So was her companion. So much for his hunch. He was letting Amanda Crowe get to him. Letting her mess with his mind. A sliver of doubt worked its way under his skin, just as she had. What if he was wrong?

Amanda had almost raced from the café at the sight and sound of the baby. But wouldn't that

have been the reaction of any grieving mother
whose baby had been kidnapped?

The voice in the darkness startled him. He spotted two figures at the end of the alley in the shadows, one large, one small. He flattened himself
against the rough rock wall, hoping they hadn't
seen him.

"You *have* to do this," the man said quietly,
urgently. "*We* have to do this. There is no going
back now."

Jesse had heard the voice somewhere before but
couldn't place it.

"Don't pressure me," the woman snapped back.
"I'll do it. I just need more time."

This voice Jesse recognized immediately.
Amanda Crowe. But who had she met in the alley?
And what did she need more time to do?

"We don't have time," the man said, sounding
frustrated and angry with her. "Stop stalling. You
know what's at stake. Just do it. Get it over with.
Tonight."

Jesse heard the sound of hurried footfalls headed
in his direction. He held his breath as the man
stomped past him. In the light bleeding out into the
alley from one of the open doorways, Jesse got a
look at him. Even from the back, he recognized
Gage Ferraro, the man who'd fathered Amanda's
baby.

He swore under his breath and waited, pressed

to the rock wall, expecting Amanda to follow her former lover. After a few minutes when she didn't appear, he glanced down the alley only to find she was gone.

He stood for a moment longer, thinking about what he'd overheard. What was Gage Ferraro doing back in town? The answer was obvious. The kidnapping. Gage and Amanda must have cooked up a plot to fleece her father. Jesse couldn't imagine anything more dangerous. Or lucrative.

He headed down the alley to where he'd left his bike, amazed at this woman. Amazed even more that he still found her intriguing. And, against his better judgment, incredibly desirable. It defied logic.

A figure suddenly stepped out of a doorway a few feet in front of him, snapping him out of his troubling thoughts. Startled, he almost pulled the piece he kept at his back before he recognized the silhouette.

Five feet four inches of spitfire, Amanda Crowe stood with her hands cocked on her hips, her feet apart, her body language nothing short of enraged.

Physically, he could have taken her with one hand tied behind him. And lord knows he wanted to take her, all right. However, Jesse was a lot of things, but he wasn't stupid. If he touched her, he'd be dead before daylight.

Nor was he about to underestimate her. Quite

frankly, he thought her as ruthless as her father. More so, after what he'd heard tonight. As she stepped closer, he could see her hair, thick and wheat-colored, cropped to her arrogant chin and her eyes, light brown with an edge to them that could cut like the shattered glass of a beer bottle.

Even if she hadn't been J.B.'s daughter he'd have taken her seriously. But she was the pride and joy of the biggest mobster this side of the Rio Grande and messing with her was messing with more than trouble.

"What the hell do you think you're doing spying on me?" she demanded.

Oh, she was something. Righteous and raging. He gave her his best grin, one that had gotten him out of a lot of tight spots. He might as well have spit in her eye for all the good it did.

"Does my father *know* you're spying on me?" she demanded, raising one fine brow.

He wiped the grin off his face and glared at her. "What do *you* think?"

She regarded him, taking his measure and making it clear she found him wanting. Some people thought his dark looks intimidating, even dangerous. But it was obvious, she wasn't one of those people.

"I think," she said dragging out each word, "that Daddy made a mistake. Surely he can do better than sending a *chauffeur*." She brushed past him, one soft, full breast grazing his bare arm, her scent lingering on his skin long after she was gone.

He stood, his back to her as she retreated down the alley. Slowly he released the breath he'd been holding, his body vibrating with a combination of lust and disgust. How the hell could he want a woman he so despised?

Had she known what she was doing just now when she'd brushed against him? Had she known the effect it would have on him? He shook his head and smiled wryly. If he was right about her, they were both playing dangerous games, risking everything. The difference was, she was a Crowe and the odds were always stacked in their favor.

He rubbed the back of his neck and stopped smiling, suddenly aware of that distinctive prickle along his spine, the one that warned him someone was behind him, watching him.

Had she stopped up the alley to look back? Not likely. The woman hadn't given him the time of day since he went to work for her father several weeks before. No, he thought, as he quickly turned, his hand going to the small of his back and his piece.

But the alley was empty. And yet he'd have sworn someone had been there just a few moments before. Gage?

Paranoia. It went with the job. He walked to his bike, swung his leg over and started the motor. It purred in the hot darkness. He considered for a moment what J.B. would do if his precious daughter told him the chauffeur had been spying on her, lusting after her. But worse, if Jesse's instincts had been right a few moments ago, then someone had been spying on him as well. Might even suspect what he was up to. That thought was enough to give him nightmares.

He cruised back to the Crowe estate, jumpy and irritable. The guard buzzed him in. He took the service road through the trees and went straight up to his apartment over the garage. On the way home, he'd invented a plausible story just in case he needed one, although in that case, he doubted he'd live long enough to tell it. But J.B. wasn't waiting for him. Nor any of the mobster's henchmen.

As he slipped his key into the lock, he noticed the corner of a piece of paper sticking out from under his door. Cautiously, he turned the key.

The piece of paper appeared to be a photocopy of a newspaper article. Frowning, he picked it up, pushed open his door and reached for the light switch. The headline leapt off the page: Infant Abandoned Beside Road.

He stepped into the apartment, locking the door behind him and read the story.

A baby had been discovered in the wee hours of the morning north of Dallas along a dirt road. The abandoned infant's parents hadn't been found yet. Police were making enquiries.

Could the baby be Susannah Crowe? Had Amanda and Gage abandoned the baby beside a road and pretended the infant had been kidnapped?

He tried to imagine a woman that cold-blooded. Amanda Crowe, he reminded himself, was a mobster's daughter. This mystery baby could be Susannah.

He glanced at the name of the town in the article. Red River, Texas? He'd never heard of it. There was no date on the article. Nor any way of knowing in what paper the story had run.

Why had someone put it under his door unless they wanted him to know what had happened to Susannah?

A thought rattled past like a freight train. If someone really did have information about Susannah Crowe, why tell the chauffeur? Unless—

His heart jackhammered and he felt oddly light-headed. Unless someone knew why he'd followed Amanda tonight. The same someone he'd sensed in the alley earlier? Someone who knew exactly what Jesse was doing here.

He moved to the window and parted the curtains, startled. Amanda's light was on in her room and she was standing at the window, staring in his direction as if waiting for him to look out. Had she put the article under his door? A cry for help. Or a dare? Catch me if you can. Was she that sure he couldn't?

Her light snapped off.

He stared at the dark window, wondering what the hell was going on, suddenly terrified of the answer.

Chapter Two

Amanda stood in the dark, telling herself Jesse couldn't possibly know. But he'd been in the alley. He might have overheard her and Gage. She tried to remember exactly what had been said. Nothing about Susannah. At least not by name.

And even if Jesse did suspect something, what could he do about it? Go to her father with his vague suspicions? She realized with a start, that was exactly what he would do. Her father's men would do anything for him, including spy on her. Jesse was no different.

In his simmering dark-eyed look she'd seen more than raw hunger. She'd seen contempt. His look said he knew her. Knew her every secret. Her every thought. Could see into her heart and see things that repulsed him.

Damn the man! She tried to calm herself, but couldn't still the shaking inside her. How dare he judge her, let alone track her down like a dog? Did he hope to get something on her he could use to get closer to her father? Or something to use as leverage to get her into his bed?

She understood men like him only too well. He'd take advantage of any opportunity. Had she given him the one he needed? She'd been so careful. Everything so deliberate, so calculated. She had tried to think like her father. The thought made her shudder. But she *was* her father's daughter, wasn't she?

Her father, she thought grimly. It would be like him to tell the chauffeur to follow her and report where she'd gone, whom she'd met. But why the chauffeur when J.B. had an assortment of trained thugs?

It definitely raised the question: had her father asked Jesse to follow her tonight? Or had Jesse done it on his own?

She hugged herself, fear making her weak at the thought that her father might know what she'd done. Had she messed up somehow, left a trail that would lead back to her and eventually destroy her?

Worse, she knew she'd passed the point of no return. She couldn't turn back now. It was too late. She had to go through with it. To the end.

She shuddered at the thought of how it could end. Especially now that she had Jesse after her. Across the courtyard she could see the window of the chauffeur's quarters clearly from her room.

He'd turned out his lights as she had. Was he looking out just as she was? Staring at her as she'd often caught him doing before?

She trembled, aware that more than fear and anger coursed through her veins tonight. As she pressed her fingers to the cool glass, her body ached for something she knew she'd never had, something she couldn't even put words to. This ache had nothing to do with her baby daughter or the trouble she was in and everything to do with the sultry Texas night and the man across the courtyard. How stupid she'd been to brush against him. Taunting him had been a very big mistake.

She hadn't expected to feel anything when she touched him but revulsion. But he'd made her long for release, a powerful, purely physical need that ignored what also simmered between them, mutual contempt and mistrust. Worse, he made her feel vulnerable.

Crowes never let themselves be vulnerable. Ever.

She'd have to do something about him. Something drastic. After all, she was her father's daughter. And he'd taught her that the world revolved around her. She could have anything she wanted. Do anything she wanted. It was the unlimited credit card that came with being his only child— and a daughter, at that. And she'd never needed that credit line more than she did right now.

She forced all thoughts of Jesse Brock from her mind and concentrated on a much more pressing problem. Her father. If he had ordered the chauffeur to follow her, then did he know something or was he just being protective?

Either way, she didn't like it.

A light knock at her bedroom door made her jump. She stood perfectly still, not making a sound. Go away.

"Miss?" Eunice Fox called through the closed door.

Hurriedly Amanda climbed into her huge poster bed, having long outgrown the frilly decor her father had insisted on, and pulled the covers over her to hide the fact that she was still fully clothed.

"Miss?" the housekeeper persisted.

Amanda didn't answer. Whatever it was, it could wait until morning.

"Miss, it's your father," Eunice said more forcefully. "He insists on speaking to you. Even if I have to wake you."

Amanda heard Eunice start to open the door and swore under her breath. "Tell him I'll be right down." She waited until she heard Eunice's retreating steps on the tile hallway, before she flung back the covers.

Her father didn't allow locks in the house, except for his wing, which was off-limits to everyone, including staff and Amanda.

Her father's security system allowed little privacy, something she only recently had come to hate. The irony of her father's idea of security didn't elude her. For all the house's hidden cameras and state-of-the-art surveillance equipment, the place made her feel anything but secure and yet allowed secrets. More secrets than even her father knew. She hoped.

Hurriedly she stripped, then dressed in a nightgown, robe and slippers. As she stepped to the door, she wondered what could be so important that he would have her awakened at this time of the night. Her footsteps slowed. News of Susannah? Her heart drummed heavy in her chest. Dear God.

She braced herself for bad news. Very bad news.

THE MOMENT Jesse walked into the late-night coffee shop and spotted Dylan Garrett, he saw the former cop's concerned expression.

"What's wrong?" Dylan asked before Jesse could sit down.

Jesse slid the now bagged copy of the newspaper article across the scarred Formica table and motioned for the waitress to bring him a cup of coffee. As Dylan read the short news article, Jesse studied the man across from him. They were about the same age but as different as night and day in both looks and temperament.

Dylan Garrett was a cowboy, rugged, muscular and tanned from hours spent on his ranch. His light-brown hair was sun streaked and he had laugh lines around his blue eyes and a dimple when he smiled, which was often.

But as Dylan looked up from the article, he wasn't smiling, let alone laughing. "Who gave you this?"

Jesse shook his head. The coffee shop was empty except for a male cook in the back and the waitress. Both looked tired and distracted. Neither was within earshot. "I found it under my door."

Dylan frowned. He'd been one hell of a cop before he quit the force to return home to the ranch and Jesse trusted him with his life. "Then someone on the Crowe compound gave it to you?"

Jesse's nodded. "It has to have something to do with the Crowe baby."

The waitress put a cup of coffee as black and thick as mud in front of him. The pot must have been on the burner for hours, turning the brew to sludge. He picked it up and took a swallow. It was god-awful stuff but he noticed that Dylan had already downed his and was working on a second cup. The man was as tough as he looked.

"Why *would* someone give it to you?" Dylan asked. "Unless your cover is blown."

"Amanda caught me following her tonight." He hated to admit it.

Dylan looked worried. "She'll go straight to her father," he said with certainty. No one knew more about J. B. Crowe than Dylan. He'd spent a year of his life working undercover for the mob.

"Yeah, I figure she will." At the very least, she'd try to get him fired. At the most... "What if the newspaper article is her way of telling me she did something with the baby?"

"Good Lord," Dylan said and shook his head. "Pull out now. I know J. B. Crowe. You're as good as dead if he finds out who you are and what you're up to."

That wasn't exactly news to Jesse but he was too close to back out now. "There is a chance that she'll slip up and make a mistake now that she suspects I'm on to her."

"Don't forget who you're dealing with here," Dylan said with obvious distaste. "On the surface, J.B. might seem like any other successful businessman. But believe me, he's into a lot more than just running numbers and racketeering. I saw and heard things—" He looked away. "Pretending to be one of them, I got to the point where I didn't know who I was. Or where the real me began or that other Dylan ended. These people are more dangerous than you think. Before they kill you, they expose you to a way of life that leaves you empty inside, without hope. If people like this can thrive around us and we can't stop them—"

"We can stop them." But he knew what Dylan was saying. For men like J. B. Crowe there were no rules. And no consequences. He called the shots; there was no higher power. And sometimes Jesse did wonder if there was any way to bring down a man like J. B. Crowe. Or his daughter. "We *will* stop them."

Dylan smiled. "I once believed that."

Jesse changed the subject to something more pleasant. "Tell me about your ranch. The Double G, right? I heard about the business you started there with your sister. How is Lily, anyway?"

"Bossy as ever."

"And Finders Keepers?" Jesse asked, more than a little interested in the detective agency Dylan and Lily had opened last fall.

"Keeps us busy," Dylan said modestly. Jesse had heard it was very successful.

"I was hoping you'd do a little investigating into this," he said, picking up the bagged article again. "I'd do it myself but I can't leave right now. Even if this baby isn't Susannah, there has to be some connection."

Dylan looked skeptical as he picked up the bagged newspaper clipping. "I should be able to track down the article and find out whether or not the baby is the missing Crowe infant. Anything else?"

"See if there are any other fingerprints on the

copy other than mine. I'd like to know who gave it to me.'' He hesitated. ''One more thing, I overheard Amanda talking to Gage Ferraro in the alley tonight. I think the two of them are working together. Maybe trying to ransom the baby.''

''Just when you think things can't get any worse.'' He shook his head. He looked tired and worried.

''Any news on that friend of yours from college?'' Jesse asked, remembering hearing about Julie Cooper's disappearance.

Dylan shook his head.

Jesse felt the clock was ticking. Since he'd gone undercover only a few weeks before, the Crowe grandchild had been kidnapped. He felt as if he were sitting on a powder keg that was about to blow.

Dylan finished his coffee and got to his feet. ''I'll get back to you on the newspaper article by tomorrow afternoon.''

Jesse rose and shook his hand. ''Thanks.''

The cowboy just nodded. ''In the meantime, mind what I say about watching your back. J. B. Crowe loves money and power but family means everything to him. When Amanda tells him you've been tailing her, you're a dead man. And she will tell him.''

Chapter Three

The moment Amanda saw her father, she knew it wasn't going to be good. He stood in the main room amid the heavy masculine western decor, his back to her and the door, his stance rigid, anxious. She knew he wouldn't have called her down this late unless something was terribly wrong.

She braced herself, glad at least that her stepmother Olivia, distraught over Susannah's kidnapping, had taken off on a shopping spree in New York. Olivia only seemed to make matters worse when J.B. was in one of his moods.

"Daddy?" Amanda asked, the childhood endearment now sounding all wrong, as if she'd aged overnight and everything had changed. The realization surprised her: she was no longer J.B.'s little girl. Had he realized that yet?

J. B. Crowe wasn't a tall man, just barely five foot ten inches, but he was extremely fit, trim and athletic, making him appear much larger, much more powerful. She'd never feared her father. Until recently.

He turned, his dark eyes warming only slightly at the sight of her. He wore one of his favorite tailored suits as he always did when he went into Dallas for dinner. She suspected he'd gone because he knew the governor was in town, probably had known where the governor would dine just so he could run into him.

She felt a shiver, aware that he believed Governor Thomas Kincaid had kidnapped Susannah. She was glad she'd begged off dinner. She hated scenes.

But she also couldn't keep kidding herself. Time was running out. It might have already run out.

"Is anything wrong?" he asked frowning.

She surfaced from her thoughts, pasting a smile on her face as she stepped to him, hurriedly giving him the perfunctory kiss on the cheek before moving behind the bar to make herself a drink, putting as much distance as she could between them. The realization surprised her. Saddened her. They had once been so close.

"I'm fine," she said quickly, filling a glass with ice. "I was worried about you since Eunice said you wanted to see me. It's so late."

"I'm sorry, my dear," he said, not sounding sorry in the least. "I hope I didn't wake you."

"No." He knew he hadn't awakened her. She suspected he knew a lot more than that.

She looked down at the array of liquor bottles. Her hand suddenly shook, the ice in her glass rattling faintly.

"Here, let me do that." He took the glass from her and stepped behind the bar, forcing a closeness that made her feel trapped, his intent gaze unnerving. Did he know what she'd done? Worse, what she planned to do next?

Her heart drummed. "Maybe just a club soda," she said, moving out of his way. "My stomach is a little upset." At least that wasn't a lie but then lying came as naturally as breathing for Crowes, didn't it? Unfortunately, she wasn't half as good as her father and she knew it.

"You're feeling well, I mean, as well as can be expected under the circumstances?" he enquired still studying her.

She'd always been his pride and joy. His precious princess. The thought turned her stomach because it had been a role she'd been happy to play. Until recently.

She met his gaze and felt tears rush into her eyes. Now wasn't the time to think about all that she'd lost. Or how much more she stood to lose. She nodded, unable to speak.

He reached for her hand and squeezed it, then handing her the glass of club soda, he led her over to the dark leather couch and motioned for her to sit down.

She cupped the cold sweating glass in her hands, her heart a drum in her chest, and waited for him to tell her that he knew everything.

"Gage is back in town," he said at last.

Her head jerked up. She'd anticipated the worst. But this completely threw her. He knew that Gage Ferraro, the son of her father's sworn enemy and Susannah's natural father, was back in town? Part of Gage's attraction had been his good looks. And the fact that her father despised him even more than he did Gage's father, Mickie Ferraro. But Gage, it appeared, had had his own agenda. She knew now that he had never cared anything for her and suspected the seduction had been to get at J.B. in some way. She'd been played for a fool and put her father in a very precarious situation. But she believed Gage did care about his daughter, Susannah. She had to believe that.

She'd only seen Gage a few times. A few times too many, she thought, unable still to remember the night she'd conceived Susannah. Gage told her later that she'd drunk too much. But she'd suspected he had put something in her drink. Otherwise she was sure she never would have slept with the man.

But she had Susannah, and Gage was gone from her life as if he'd never existed, so she had no regrets. She would just be much more careful in the future. Had she told her father, Amanda had no doubt he would have killed Gage. She suspected all that stopped him when he found out about the pregnancy was rumor of an investigation into some of his so-called business deals. Also, the Organization wouldn't have liked it. At first J.B. had threatened a shotgun wedding, but Amanda had known her father wasn't about to let Gage become his son-in-law. Gage's loyalties were to his father, a competing mobster boss who had been trying to take over some of J.B.'s territories. He'd never let a man he didn't trust marry into the family.

So with the promise of peace, her father had seen that Gage was given a job in Chicago and literally escorted out of town within hours. No one had asked Amanda what she wanted. J.B. always knew what was best for her and the baby.

She said nothing now, waiting for the other shoe to drop.

"Gage believes he can find Susannah and bring down Kincaid," her father said, a note of grudging respect in his voice.

She stared at him, dumbstruck. Why hadn't Gage told her this? And yet it was so like Gage. Pretending to get into her father's good graces by bringing Susannah home safely—and seeing that Kincaid took the rap for the kidnapping. Why hadn't she thought that Gage might pull something like this?

"While Gage is in town," J.B. said, "I want you to stay away from him."

There was a severity to her father's voice that surprised her. He thought she'd go to Gage. Probably already knew she had, thanks to Jesse.

"You're not to see him under any circumstances." Her father smiled, lightening his tone. "As a favor to me. And only because it's for your own good."

As if he knew what was good for her. She would have reminded him that she was twenty-five, of legal age, and that she would decide who she saw and what she did. But she'd only dated Gage Ferraro to show her father that he couldn't tell her what to do, a childish, stupid thing to have done. She'd underestimated Gage and paid the price.

The truth was, she had never known independence, having lived her entire life under her father's roof, under his rules, and she never would, if he had his way.

She gave him what she hoped was a reassuring smile, not feeling in the least bit guilty for lying to him. "It's not a problem."

He returned her smile but she noticed it never reached his eyes. He hadn't forgiven her for Gage. He saw it as a betrayal and her father did not forgive easily. Even his own daughter. Especially his own daughter.

"Good," he said. "Then there is nothing to worry about. Soon Susannah will be home, Kincaid will be neutralized and we can put all of this behind us." His eyes narrowed. He knew her too well. "Are you ill, my dear? Maybe it was something you ate? I understand you went out tonight and only recently returned. I do hope you're getting enough rest."

She felt shaken. She'd taken care of the guard at the gate—and the cameras. She'd even waited until Eunice and the other hired help had gone to bed. The only way her father could have known that she'd left and gone to a café was if Jesse had already reported to her father.

The bastard. "I met a friend," she said and waited for J.B. to ask the friend's name and if he knew her. When he didn't, she knew he'd had the chauffeur, of all people, follow her. That was a new low, even for her father.

"I hope you had Jesse take you in the car," he said, killing any question in her mind. Why did anything her father do still shock her?

"No, actually, I drove the BMW."

He raised a brow. "Not the Mercedes convertible I got you for your birthday?"

She felt her heart rate quicken. Why did he care which car she took unless— She felt sick. Had he put some sort of tracking device on the Mercedes? Or had he wanted her to use it because it was parked in the garage near the chauffeur's quarters?

"I just felt like driving the BMW," she managed to reply. "For old times' sake."

He nodded, still watching her, reminding her of when she was a child and he suspected she was lying. "I don't like the idea of you going out alone. Not after what happened with Susannah—" He stopped, his gaze boring into her. "I couldn't bear it if anything were to happen to you."

She felt a chill, his words a warning she couldn't ignore. She had betrayed him once. She was not to do it again.

"Don't worry," she said quietly. "I am always very careful." Now she would be even more careful. "But if it makes you feel better, I will have Jesse drive me."

That seemed to satisfy him. At least temporarily. He patted her shoulder. He didn't ask her anything else about tonight. Obviously he already knew. Damn Jesse Brock.

"You didn't ask if I'd received a ransom note yet," he said, catching her off guard.

"Have you?" she asked, sounding breathless, sounding scared.

"No," he said studying her. "Odd isn't it? Unless Susannah has been kidnapped for some other reason."

"What other reasons are there besides money and power?" she asked.

He smiled at that. "None, that I can think of. But don't you worry, my dear, I will get my granddaughter back. One way or the other."

Trembling at the certainty she heard in his voice, she kissed her father's cheek and left him to finish his drink alone, acutely aware that he was suspicious of her comings and goings. Hopefully he just thought she was meeting Gage Ferraro behind his back. That was much safer than the truth.

She hurried up to her room, not turning on the light as she went to the window. The darkness smelled of hyacinths, the air sweet and sweltering. She closed the curtains and went into the bathroom where she'd long ago disabled the surveillance camera.

Still shaking, she pulled out the equipment she would need, then pushed it back into its hiding place. Not tonight. No matter what Gage said. It was too dangerous. Tomorrow night. Her last chance. She'd do it then.

Her heart beat faster. If she failed tomorrow night—

She refused to consider that possibility. Too much was at stake. Tomorrow night. Come hell or high water. Or even Jesse Brock.

Across the courtyard, the light glowed in his

apartment and she could see him moving behind the curtains, a shadow as dark as the man himself.

With a lot of luck and every ounce of deceitful Crowe blood that ran through her veins, she would see that no one ever found out what had really happened to her baby, especially her father. Jesse Brock didn't know it yet, but he was going to help her. It would be his last good deed.

THE PHONE RANG, making Jesse jump. He stopped pacing and reached for it, expecting the worst.

"Bring my car around," J.B. ordered and hung up.

Jesse looked at the clock, instantly uneasy. J.B. seldom went out this late. And yet, Jesse had been expecting trouble. Amanda had obviously told her father that he'd followed her tonight and now the old man wanted to go for a ride. Great.

Jesse figured he had two options: Run. Or stay and tough it out. In which case, he wanted to take a weapon. But he knew that would be the wrong thing to do. If one of J.B.'s goons frisked him... No, it would be better to play it straight. Even when the old man got around to asking Jesse about earlier tonight.

He took a breath and let it out slowly, then he went to get the car.

As he pulled up in front of the house, J.B. came out with his two bodyguards, two big bruisers with pug faces and bad attitudes whom Jesse had nicknamed Death and Destruction. It was no secret that neither man liked him. Probably because Jesse had been able to gain J.B.'s trust so quickly.

It had been a simple setup. Wait until Amanda and her father got out of their car at J.B.'s favorite restaurant. Add one speeding, out-of-control car and a chauffeur waiting by his boss's car who just happened to be able to jump in at the right moment and save the damsel in distress.

Shocked and grateful, Crowe had played right into his hands. He'd hired Jesse away from his "former" boss with a substantial raise and the rest was history. The almost hit-and-run had happened so fast Death and Destruction hadn't even had a chance to move, something Crowe had never let them forget. They'd hated Jesse ever since.

Jesse got out of the large, freshly waxed and polished Lincoln to open the back door for his boss. Death, the slimmer of the two, slid in, followed by J.B., then Destruction. Not one of them even gave Jesse a second glance.

As he closed the door and went around to the driver's seat, he wondered if that was a bad sign. With men who would kill him without a moment's hesitation behind him, he began to sweat as he waited for instructions.

"Johnson Park," J.B. ordered.

Jesse shifted into gear and got the car moving,

not liking the sound of this. Johnson Park was an old industrial area outside of Dallas that had been closed for a good twenty years, maybe more. Not a good place to go this time of the night. It was the kind of place you could dispose of a body too easily.

Prolonging the trip was out of the question. Traffic was light and Johnson Park wasn't far. He drove, acutely aware of the men in the back seat and the position he'd put himself in.

When he slowed for the park, he glanced in his rearview mirror and wished he hadn't. The old man met his gaze and what Jesse saw there turned his blood to block ice.

He pulled into the park. The night was black, no stars, no moon, only an occasional unbroken streetlight along the long rows of abandoned warehouses. He drove to the end of the row J.B. indicated and stopped, turned off the lights and killed the engine, unconsciously holding his breath, waiting for the distinct sound of the slide on a weapon being readied.

"Stay here," the mobster ordered him as the two goons opened their doors and J.B. slid out of the car.

Inside the dark stillness of the car, Jesse released the breath he'd been holding, his relief so intense he felt sick to his stomach. He took a few long breaths and tried to quiet his banging heart. That had felt too close. And he still wasn't out of the woods.

It took a moment for his eyes to adjust. A single bulb burned in a building off to his right, in the same direction J.B. and the two bodyguards had gone. A dark-colored Cadillac was parked at the edge of the building.

What the hell were they doing out here at this time of the night? And, although he didn't recognize the Cadillac, he had a bad feeling it had something to do with him.

After a few moments, he cautiously popped open his door and slipped out, closing it quietly behind him. As he moved through the darkness toward the light, he heard J.B.'s voice raised in anger. He crept along the side of the building, following the sound. Above him he could see a broken, dirty window. Cautiously, he climbed up onto a pile of old crates and peered in through the opening in the glass. He could see nothing but shadows and dark shapes off to the left but he could hear J.B. still talking.

"You're telling me that you didn't know this guy you saw her with?" J.B. demanded, his tone hard enough to crack concrete.

"I told you, I didn't get a good look at him. It was dark. It was an alley for hell's sake and I had to get out of there or Amanda would have seen me watching her." The voice had a distinct whine to it. A very familiar whine.

"What I don't understand is what you were doing there in the first place," J.B. said evenly.

"Look, I leveled with you. I'm going to find your granddaughter for you. Nothing's changed. The only reason I called you was to let you know what I'd seen. As a favor. So what is this all about, getting me down here tonight, interrogating me like this?" Gage Ferraro demanded.

Gage had seen Jesse and Amanda in the alley earlier. That much was clear. But if Amanda had told her father about her encounter with Jesse, this should have been old news. Unless she hadn't told him. Yet.

"I just want to make sure your plans don't change," the mobster warned. "I don't want you having anything to do with my daughter. Or my granddaughter."

"Hey, we're talking about my daughter, here," Gage said. The soft scuff of soles on the concrete drowned out whatever J.B. said back to him.

Suddenly all four men came into view beneath the stark light of the single bulb hanging from the rafters.

Destruction had Gage in a headlock and J.B. was close enough to Gage to steal his breath.

"You have no rights to that child," J.B. said in

a tone that curdled Jesse's blood. "I thought we agreed to that?"

Gage was trying to nod.

"As far as I'm concerned," J.B. was saying, his voice low and as dangerous as Jesse had ever heard it, "you have no daughter and you don't know mine, either. Is that understood?"

"Yeah, yeah, J.B.," Gage croaked.

Destruction released him.

Gage rubbed his throat. "I told you," he said, sounding hoarse. "I'm going to do this for you. As a favor. That's all."

J.B. nodded. "Let's hope for your sake you're telling me the truth."

Gage looked worried.

J.B. patted Gage on the face. "Find my grand-daughter." The mobster turned and walked toward the door, but stopped at the sound of his cell phone ringing. He motioned for Death and Destruction to go on ahead of him with Gage, then reached in his pocket and pulled out the phone.

"Yes?" he barked, then listened. "You got Diana? Does Kincaid know yet? Good." He smiled as he snapped the phone shut and put it back in his pocket. "So now Governor, I have *your* daughter and soon to be born grandchild. How does it feel?"

Jesse winced as if he'd been kicked in the stomach. Crowe had kidnapped the governor's daughter, Diana. The governor's pregnant daughter.

He swore under his breath and he jumped down from the crate and ran along the edge of the building. He knew how dangerous it would be for Diana and her unborn baby to be taken in retaliation for Susannah's kidnapping.

There was no love lost between J. B. Crowe and Governor Thomas Kincaid, not since the governor had declared war on the mob in Texas. But Jesse suspected there was something else between J.B. and Thomas, something more personal.

Hurriedly, Jesse ran along the edge of the building. He could see the Lincoln and knew he couldn't reach it in time. Nor could he let Gage see him again.

Jesse stopped at the corner of the building, caught. He watched as Gage went straight to the dark-colored Caddy. The driver hopped out as if surprised to see Gage back so soon. It was obvious he'd been asleep, Jesse realized with silent thanks. There was a good chance the driver hadn't seen Jesse get out of the Lincoln then.

Gage climbed into the back of his Cadillac and the driver closed the door.

J.B. stood with Death and Destruction as if waiting for Gage to leave. Gage looked as if he couldn't wait to get away as his driver climbed back into the front of the car and started it.

Forgetting about Gage, Jesse considered the spot he found himself in. There wasn't any way he could get to the Lincoln without J.B. seeing him. For a moment, he actually considered just taking off and not looking back.

But blowing his own cover now, when he was so close, wasn't his style. He'd bluffed his way into the chauffeur job, he could bluff his way through this. He hoped.

Gage's driver gave the Caddy a little too much gas as he left. Jesse saw J.B. smile in the glare of the Cadillac's headlights. About then, however, J.B. seemed to notice that his own driver wasn't at his post, and the smile faded.

Jesse ambled out from the dark edge of the building and walked leisurely toward the Lincoln.

"I thought I told you to stay in the car?" J.B.'s voice sounded at once suspicious and furious.

"I had to take a leak," Jesse snapped and moved ahead of the mobster to open his door. He could feel J.B.'s gaze on him and looked up to meet the man's dark eyes without flinching. It took all his nerve.

J.B. held his gaze for a long heart-stopping moment, then he shook his head as if in disgust or disbelief, and slid into the back seat. *It's so hard to get good help these days,* Jesse thought sarcastically.

Death slid in beside the mobster and Destruction

strutted around to the other side, giving Jesse a smug grin that hinted that he was looking forward to the day that he got to kill Jesse.

Jesse had made it a point to never be cowed by J.B., but it was getting harder and harder not to let the mobster see him sweat.

''Home,'' J.B. ordered the moment Jesse slipped into the driver's seat.

Still shaking inside, he gripped the wheel and drove. He didn't dare look in the rearview mirror again. No one said a word from the back seat.

Jesse tried to relax but he couldn't forget how close he'd come to having his cover blown. Gage Ferraro had seen him talking to Amanda in the alley earlier. Fortunately, Gage hadn't gotten a good look at him.

But now Jesse wasn't sure how long his luck would hold. It seemed he and Gage were looking for the same thing. Amanda's baby, Susannah. And even if, as Jesse suspected, Gage was lying through his teeth to Crowe, their paths were bound to cross again. And it was just a matter of time before Gage recognized Jesse as the cop who'd arrested him for drug possession three years ago.

Chapter Four

The phone rang early the next morning, jerking Jesse from a not so sound sleep.

J.B.'s deep voice filled the line. "I won't be needing your services today but should Amanda want to go anywhere, I want you to take her. I don't want her driving herself. Do you understand me?"

"Yes, sir," he said, heart pounding.

"By the way, I appreciate you keeping an eye on my daughter last night when she went out again."

He swore softly under his breath and sat up, suddenly wide awake. "Yes?"

But J.B. hung up without another word, leaving Jesse off balance. Had Amanda told him just as Jesse and Dylan had known she would? Or had J.B. just figured it out from what Gage had reported to him? The guard at the gate hadn't been at his post but the surveillance cameras would have picked up both Amanda—and Jesse right behind her. Still, Crowe couldn't know that Jesse had followed Amanda to the café.

Either way, it did not bode well. But why would J.B. order him to drive Amanda? Why didn't J.B. fire him? Or have him killed? And why hadn't he asked him to report back on where Amanda went? Maybe J.B. had Gage for that. Or at least J.B. thought he did.

One false move, Jesse knew, and he was toast. Who was he kidding? His cover could already be blown wide-open. He could be living on borrowed time and just not know it. J.B. was probably setting him up. Giving him enough rope to hang himself.

He shook his head, amazed at the spot he found himself in this morning. Right between Amanda and her old man, a very dangerous place to be.

But in the meantime... He tried to still his racing heart. Amanda couldn't leave the Crowe estate without him. He couldn't help but grin, thinking how furious that must make her. Would she be angry enough to finally show her hand? He could only hope.

While he knew he could be walking into a trap J.B. had laid for him, Jesse still felt pretty cocky as he headed for the shower. This might prove to be just the break he'd been waiting for. If he was right, and Amanda and Gage had done something with the baby, then she must be running scared now that her father had people spying on her. She'd try to cover her tracks. She'd slip up. And when she did, Jesse would be there to nail her. So to speak.

He drowned that thought in a cold shower, disgusted with himself because of his body's reaction to the woman. Afterward, he called the main house to let Amanda know he'd be available to drive her and maybe to rub it in a little. He could only assume that she'd tried to get him fired. Or killed. And had failed. At least temporarily. He was feeling pretty pleased about that.

But he couldn't get his call past the housekeeper. Ms. Crowe, Eunice said, wasn't up yet.

He polished several of J. B. Crowe's fleet of expensive cars, watching for any sign of life behind Amanda's closed curtains. None.

As he worked, he found his thoughts divided between worrying that Amanda might have found a way to sneak out without him noticing, and trying to make sense of the newspaper clipping that had been slipped under his door last night. It had to have been someone inside the estate who'd given it to him. He ticked off the few hired help who lived on the premises.

Not the tiny, gray-haired Eunice Fox who'd been with the Crowe family for years. Nor Consuela Ruiz, the family cook. Nor the gardener, a withered, little old man named Malcolm Hines, who had been one of J.B.'s first bodyguards.

Jesse couldn't imagine any of them being disloyal to J.B. or any member of his family. And not just for fear of their lives. That left only Death and Destruction, but Jesse doubted either of them even knew how to read.

So who did that leave? J.B. Not likely. And Amanda.

Jesse called the house again after lunch.

"Ms. Crowe isn't up," Eunice informed him in a tone that dared him to insinuate that it wasn't Amanda's right to sleep all day if she so desired. He knew the housekeeper had been up for hours working and wondered how she could be so protective of such a spoiled, young woman who had never worked a day in her life and no doubt ever would.

"Should she get up—"

"I'll let her know you're available," the elderly woman cut him off icily. "I'm sure she will appreciate knowing that." She hung up, convincing Jesse that Eunice definitely hadn't been the one who'd put the copy of the newspaper clipping under his door.

While he polished J.B.'s fancy fleet and waited for Dylan to call with news on the baby, Jesse found himself thinking about Gage Ferraro and wondering what Amanda saw in the man. Obviously, there was no accounting for taste, but it did make Jesse wonder. Why had J.B. taken his daughter's dishonor so lightly? The J. B. Crowe Jesse had come to know would have had Gage swimming with the fish in cement shoes at the bottom of White Rock Lake.

Jesse wondered what J.B. would do if he found out that Amanda was consorting with the enemy again? If Gage and Amanda had kidnapped Susannah as some sort of scam, Jesse didn't want to be around when J.B. found out.

Meanwhile, he wondered how Gage's father, Mickie Ferraro, had taken losing his first grandchild. Especially considering that he and J.B. were rumored to be fighting for control inside the Organization. Mickie and J.B. had reportedly started with the mob as little more than kids.

Gage was a two-bit hoodlum who was trying to work his way up in the mob. If he really could find Susannah and bring down Kincaid, J.B. would owe him. But somehow Jesse didn't believe that was Gage's game.

Gage Ferraro was a wild card and one Jesse didn't like seeing in the deck. And Amanda... It was just a matter of getting her in a compromising position. The thought had too much appeal—and was damn dangerous.

He just wished he could figure out how all the

pieces fit together, especially how the newspaper clipping fit into the mix.

Dylan, true to his word, contacted him a little after two. "We should meet," the cowboy said.

Jesse picked a meeting place nearby and called the main house a third time, only to be told that Ms. Crowe had finally gotten out of bed and planned to spend the day beside the pool. Mr. Crowe would be home soon. The two would be spending the rest of the afternoon and evening together. Jesse wouldn't be needed.

Anxious to hear what Dylan had discovered, he left, confident Amanda couldn't leave with her father expected home any minute.

THE SMALL Texas barbecue joint served cold beer and chipped pork sandwiches with hot sauce. Because of the time of day, the place wasn't busy. He took a table at the back so he could watch the door.

Dylan joined him ten minutes later.

"So is the baby Susannah?" Jesse asked without preamble.

To Jesse's disappointment, Dylan shook his head.

"The baby found beside the road was a boy, a newborn," Dylan said.

Jesse frowned. "Then how could the clipping be connected to Susannah Crowe's disappearance?"

"I don't think it is," Dylan said. "The baby boy left beside Woodland Lake Road just outside of Red River, Texas, had dark hair and dark eyes. He was only a few hours old, leading police to believe he was born on June 5." He paused.

Jesse felt a jolt. The baby had been born on his birthday?

"June 5," Dylan continued, "thirty years ago, 1971."

Jesse's heart took off at a sprint. He stared at the cowboy for a long moment. "June 5 is my birthday."

Dylan nodded. "I had a feeling it was. That's why I did some more checking. I couldn't find out who adopted the baby. Texas adoption laws won't allow that. So I went from the other direction." Dylan seemed to hesitate. "I checked your birth certificate."

Jesse was already shaking his head.

"I don't know how to say this, Jesse. I checked with the hospital listed as your place of birth. You weren't born in Dallas, at least not to Pete and Marie McCall."

Jesse could barely find breath to ask, "What are you saying? That you think I'm that abandoned baby?" He shook his head and rubbed the back of his neck. "I was the middle son, with two brothers and three younger sisters, the perfect family. I had this great childhood. If anything, I was my parents' favorite—'' He stopped and shook his head again, all the little things now making him doubt who he was and everything he'd once believed. ''There is no way I was adopted. There has to be some sort of mistake. Of course I was born in Dallas, just like my brothers and sisters. Why would my parents lie about where I was born?''

The answer was obvious. If he was that abandoned baby, his parents would have lied to protect him from the truth. They wouldn't want him to know that his birth mother had cared so little that she'd left him beside a dirt road in a cardboard box.

''I'm sorry, Jesse,'' Dylan said.

He looked past Dylan to the bartender punching up numbers on the jukebox. A Bob Wills and His Texas Playboys song filled the air, Texas swing. He felt sick. And scared. ''Who the hell am I, then?''

''You're still Jesse McCall, the man you've always been,'' Dylan said.

Jesse shook his head. He'd been Jesse Brock since he'd become Crowe's chauffeur two weeks ago. And now he had a bad feeling he wasn't even Jesse McCall, the person he thought he'd been for thirty years. ''I have to know.''

Dylan nodded almost sadly but didn't seem surprised. ''You realize you're probably not going to like what you uncover, if you're even able to dig up anything after all these years.''

He nodded, trying to think of a good reason a mother would abandon her baby.

"Do you want me to keep digging?" Dylan asked. "I have another case that's going to tie me up for a while but after that—"

Jesse nodded. He couldn't leave the Crowe case, not now. And after thirty years, what was a few more days?

"Then you're going to stay on the Crowe estate?" Dylan asked.

He nodded, his thoughts torn between this shocking news and Amanda Crowe. "The old man called me this morning and told me he wants me to drive her wherever Amanda wants to go. He thanked me for keeping an eye on her. And obviously someone on the Crowe estate thinks they know who I am or they wouldn't have put the newspaper clipping under my door.''

Dylan looked uneasy and Jesse nodded in agreement.

"I know I'm walking a tightrope here," Jesse acknowledged and told him about Gage Ferraro. "Now everyone is looking for Susannah, including Gage, if he isn't just stringing J.B. along. But I overheard him prodding her to make her move. I intend to be there when she does.''

Dylan studied him for a long moment and Jesse

wondered if the cowboy realized just how involved Jesse had gotten in this case.

"She's a beautiful woman," Dylan said quietly.

Jesse laughed. "She's also a Crowe and she'd cut your throat in a heartbeat."

"Just don't forget that. Jesse, I know this news about the newspaper clipping comes as a shock to you," Dylan said.

"Yeah." He loved his parents, his family and he'd always felt a part of them. This was more than a shock. He felt as if the earth under him was no longer solid. As if nothing was as it seemed.

"Take it slow, okay?" Dylan advised. "Give it a little time."

Time. Right. Too bad that wasn't his nature.

Jesse called the Crowe compound at a little after three. Mr. Crowe was with his daughter. Both had asked not to be disturbed. Nor had they changed their minds about needing Jesse's services, Eunice assured him. They would be dining in tonight together.

After he left the compound, he called his boss at the Dallas P.D. and told him what he'd overheard J.B. Crowe say the night before about the governor's daughter Diana. His boss said he'd handle it and hung up.

He had time. Enough time he could drive up to his parents' house in Pilot Point and back. It wasn't but a couple of hours. Amanda wouldn't dare try to sneak out with her father home and dinner planned for the two of them. Would she?

MARIE MCCALL MET HIM at the door, excitedly kissed him on the cheek then noticed something was wrong. "What is it, honey?"

His mother. She knew him as no one else did. Her hand went to his forehead, just as it had when he was a child.

"Are you feeling ill?" she enquired, regarding him with concern as she ushered him in.

"Stop fussing over him," Pete McCall called jovially from the kitchen. "You're just in time," he said to Jesse. "How about a beer before dinner? We were getting ready to throw some steaks on the grill."

"I made your favorite," his mother said still eyeing him. "Strawberry-rhubarb pie for dessert. I must have known you'd stop by."

"Thanks but I can't stay for dinner." Both his parents looked disappointed. "But I will take that cold beer."

He followed them to the wide redwood deck that overlooked the lake. The air was scented with fresh-mown grass, lake water and glowing briquettes beneath the grill. His father opened a bottle of cold beer and handed it to him.

Now that he was here, he felt foolish. Everything was so normal, just as it had been growing up. These were his parents. How could he doubt that? He was the middle son, wedged in neatly between Alex and Charley, with three great sisters, and this was the perfect family with the split-level house, deck, basketball hoop, horseshoe pit, lake out the back door and parents who doted on him. This was home.

He felt guilty. They were so glad to see him and he realized he hadn't been home for several months because of his undercover work. He hadn't even thought about them.

"I need to talk to you," he said, just wanting to get it out. Obviously there was some mistake. They would clear it up and he would feel foolish but they would forgive him.

They looked worried. "What is it, honey?" his mother asked, taking a seat on the arm of his father's deck chair. Her hand went to the tiny gold heart she wore on a chain around her neck. She stroked the unusual-shaped heart with her thumb, just as she always did when she was worried or upset. He knew her so well. Just as she knew him.

Still standing he took a sip of the beer, almost talking himself out of even bringing up the subject. But he had to get this settled so he could get back to his undercover assignment, get his head back where it belonged.

"I know you're going to think this is crazy…"

Was it his imagination or did his father tense? "Is there any chance I might have been adopted?"

His mother froze, her eyes suddenly swimming with tears. His father said nothing as he put an arm around her.

Oh, God. Jesse sat down heavily in one of the deck chairs, the earth beneath him no longer stable and in that moment, he knew that nothing would ever be the same. "Was I the baby found outside of Red River?" he asked when he found his voice.

Neither answered but his mother began to cry. His father looked pale, his face drawn, older than Jesse had ever seen him.

Jesse closed his eyes for a moment. "How—" He heard the strangled emotion in the word, felt the panicked knocking of his heart and struggled for his next breath. "How did you get me?" He looked from his father to his mother.

She said nothing as she reached behind her to unclasp the gold chain. He'd never known her to take if off before and for a moment, he didn't move.

She held it out to him. "I suppose it was wrong, but we never wanted you to know."

As if in a trance, he lifted his hand to take it from her. The gold chain with the heart pooled in his palm, oddly cold and heavy. He wondered if taking it off had lifted a weight from off his mother's shoulders. Or just the opposite after all these years of keeping this secret.

He looked down at the funny little heart, then at her.

"I found it in your baby blanket." Her voice broke.

He didn't know what to say. He stared down at what looked to him like a broken heart, so like his own. The memory came out of nowhere. He'd been no more than three or four when he'd asked his mother about the strange heart she wore. Her words came back to him, their meaning suddenly clear.

"I prize this heart because a special woman gave it to me," his mother had said.

He gazed at his parents now. He had never thought he looked that much different from them, from his siblings or his other relatives. He'd always been a little darker, looked a *little* dissimilar, but because he'd had no reason to think otherwise, he'd always felt like one of them. Why hadn't he noticed that he was different?

"Why did you adopt me?" he had to ask. "It wasn't like you didn't already have children."

"Because you needed us and we loved you the moment we saw you," his mother said a little too quickly as if she'd been rehearsing that line for thirty years.

He nodded, having never felt so alone, so absolutely desolate. He wondered what else they'd lied to him about. What else they were keeping from him. And who at the Crowe compound had known that he wasn't the son of Marie and Pete McCall? More important, why did they want him to know? Anyway he looked at it, he knew he was in trouble. Someone at the compound knew he wasn't who he was pretending to be. Someone knew more about him than even he knew about himself—and that scared him more than he wanted to admit.

Chapter Five

The hot Texas afternoon sun shimmered off the turquoise of the pool, but Amanda hardly noticed the sun or the water. She felt deathly cold inside and scared, more scared than she had ever been.

"Your father suggested you get some sun by the pool," Eunice had told her when she'd gone downstairs. "He thought it would do you some good. Also he asked Consuela to make your favorite dinner tonight. He'll be joining you."

Amanda recoiled as if struck by a blow. She fought not to stagger.

"If you need anything, I will be here," Eunice continued. "So will Consuela and Malcolm. The chauffeur has been dismissed for the day."

She'd stared at the gray-haired woman, too shocked to speak. J.B. had never ordered her to stay on the estate before, let alone told the hired help to spy on her.

She felt sick. This was her father's way of trying

to scare her. And she *was* scared. Because she understood the threat perfectly. Her father either knew the truth. Or suspected it.

It took everything in her not to run. But she knew the guard at the gate would be expecting that. She was trapped. All the more so because she hadn't finished what she had to do here.

So she'd spent the day beside the pool, just as her father had ordered her to do. She would play the dutiful daughter. One last time.

Eunice had come out to check on her periodically. Even Malcolm Hines, the gardener, had spent the day weeding a flower bed not far from the pool, his presence leaving little doubt that he, too, was keeping an eye on her. The only person she hadn't seen was Jesse. She'd been surprised when she heard him leave just after lunch. And as far as she knew, he hadn't returned.

Consuela, the family's longtime cook, had brought her food and drinks. But while Amanda felt closer to the cook than to her own mother, who had been about the same age as Consuela, she knew she would find no allies on the estate. And certainly none in Olivia, her stepmother, who still had not returned from her New York shopping spree.

Like Olivia, the servants were loyal only to J.B. Amanda had never understood their devotion to him and wondered now what debts these servants owed that required them to indenture themselves to him for life. Whatever the debt, she suspected they would kill for him if he asked them.

She felt like a prisoner. But when her initial shock wore off, she realized she had always been a prisoner here—she just hadn't realized it until now. Her father had manipulated her to get what he wanted: Her and then Susannah under his roof, under his thumb. She shivered, afraid what he would do if he knew about her plans.

Her only hope was to be as cold and heartless as he was should she get caught. The thought chilled her to the bone.

As the sun sank behind the oak trees, she heard the tinkle of ice. Consuela placed a tall glass on the table next to her.

"I thought you might like some lemonade, it is so hot out." The large, good-natured Mexican woman smiled warmly.

"Thank you, Consuela."

"Have you heard anything about the baby?" the woman asked in a whisper as if the kidnapper might be listening.

"Still no word," Amanda lied.

Consuela crossed herself and muttered something in Spanish that Amanda didn't understand. Something about history repeating itself. Impulsively, the cook bent to hug her fiercely, and Amanda realized Consuela was referring to when someone had tried to kidnap Amanda when she was just a baby. That's when her father had installed the security system.

"Your father will find her," Consuela said, voicing exactly what Amanda feared most. "Mr. Crowe, he always take care of his own. Look how good he take care of you."

After Consuela returned to the kitchen, Amanda heard her father's car and wasn't surprised that he'd returned early. She braced herself, determined to hide her fear of him—and the power he had over her.

IT WAS DARK and late when Jesse returned to the Crowe estate. He'd been driving aimlessly for hours, letting the wind and the dark rush past as wildly as his thoughts. He felt dazed and lost, haunted by his talk with his parents.

He'd grilled them, desperate for information about his birth parents. But both had insisted they knew little. He'd been found beside the road. They'd taken him in and later adopted him. They'd never known who his mother was. Or his birth father. They'd left Red River and never looked back. Their story never varied.

Why then did he sense they were keeping something from him? Something they couldn't bear to tell him?

His head swam. He had so many unanswered

questions. Why had his birth mother left him beside a dirt road in a cardboard box? And how was it he'd been miraculously found by Marie and Pete McCall?

He breezed up to the guard at the entrance, waited for the gate to swing open and followed the hot, melting rope of blacktop that wound through a thick-leafed arch of oaks, maples and crepe myrtles. A cool breeze seeped from the darkness under the trees.

He breathed it in, trying hard to concentrate on his job. He'd always prided himself on being able to put his personal life on hold while on assignment. That ability had only been tested a few times, however. Most recently by Amanda Crowe. And *now*—finding out that his whole life had been a lie.

Through the trees, he caught the flicker of lights from the hacienda. He slowed, not in the least bit anxious to see Amanda and let her stir him up. Not tonight. He felt torn, desperately needing the truth and yet sick that he would hurt the only parents he'd ever known. They had begged him not to try to find out who he was.

"You're our son," his father had said, his voice breaking. "Nothing is to be gained by digging in the past."

"Jesse, please don't do this," his mother had pleaded. "I don't want you to be hurt."

But he was already hurt. If only he could just let it go. Why did it have to matter?

But it did matter. It mattered a whole hell of a lot and he knew he couldn't let it alone. As soon as he found out what happened to Susannah Crowe he was going to find out about that little baby boy someone had abandoned beside the road thirty years ago.

Ahead, the trees opened a little to make room for the sprawling structures of the Crowe compound. He took the delivery road that went past the garage. The road was dark, cloaked in trees, and far enough from the house that there was little chance he'd run into any of the Crowes tonight.

The garage and his apartment loomed, large and unlit. Ahead, the trees made a dark canopy over the narrow road. Suddenly, he felt the skin on the back of his neck prickle. Something moved off to his right.

He brought the cycle to a stop in the deep shadows next to the garage and his apartment. The stifling Texas spring night quickly settled around him, heavy as hot tar. In the distance, he thought he heard music. Latin music. Coming from the main house. Coming from Amanda's room.

He'd convinced himself that he was imagining things when he spotted the dark figure skulking along the edge of the main house, headed toward the far wing of the main house. J.B.'s wing. An

area considered extremely off-limits. One even
Jesse hadn't dared explore.

He swung off the bike, intrigued, and slipped
through the pools of shadows, following the same
path the intruder had taken, wondering why the
security system hadn't picked them up yet.

J.B.'s wing ran east of the main house, stretch-
ing back into the trees. A fortress of wrought-iron
barred windows and massive wooden doors, it
would take a tank to get into without a key.

Jesse gaped in amazement to see one of the iron
grates hanging to the side and the window open.
He reached automatically for his weapon and realized belatedly that he'd left it in his apartment
when he went to see his parents.

As he neared the window, he could hear someone quietly opening and closing drawers in an adjoining room. He tried to imagine the fool who
would break into J.B.'s office. As he slipped
through the window, he tensed, waiting for the security alarm to go off.

When it didn't, he felt a cold chill run up his
spine. Whoever was in the next room had somehow disarmed the system. *Damn,* he thought as he
edged toward the faint sound of shuffling papers.
He wished he had a gun.

On the wall of the adjoining office, the narrow
beam of a flashlight flickered. It bobbed and dipped

like a firefly to the sound of drawers being opened and closed in a filing cabinet.

Jesse looked around for something to use as a weapon. A small statue of a woman near the door caught his eye. He wrapped his fist around her slim waist and carrying her like a club, edged toward the open doorway.

He shouldn't have been surprised by what he saw when he peered around the doorjamb. Nothing the woman did should still surprise him. But it did.

Amanda was bent over an old oak desk, going through the drawers.

"What the hell are you doing?" he demanded, stepping into the room.

She jumped and spun around. She had a small book in one hand, like a ledger, and a flashlight in the other.

Her eyes looked golden in the light, like a cat's. He half expected her to pounce.

She eyed him, then the statue in his hand. "It isn't what you think," she said, her voice a low purr.

The sound skittered across his skin, sending a shiver through him. "What do I think?" he managed to rasp.

She smiled then and stepped toward him, the flashlight beam a golden disk on the floor at her side.

He didn't move. Couldn't. She closed the space

between them, stopping within a hairbreadth of him. Not touching, but so close he could feel her body heat, smell her exotic, haunting scent, feel the electricity arcing between them. But it was the look in her eyes that was his downfall. The promise of all that he had longed for. And more.

"Jesse?" she breathed and she leaned up as if to kiss him.

The cold barrel of the gun in his ribs snapped him right out of the fantasy.

"Do as I say or I'll kill you," she ordered.

It had been one hell of a day. Not his best. Everything about it seemed surreal. Even comical on some level. Except for the business end of the weapon pressed into his ribs and the desperation he heard in his attacker's voice.

"I know how to use this and I will," Amanda said as she jabbed him with the gun. "You just saved me a trip to your apartment. Now let's get out of here and don't forget who you're dealing with."

Not likely. He put down the statue carefully and let her lead him at gunpoint out of the office. He might have called her bluff, but being taken her hostage was the perfect way to end the perfect day. He didn't think she'd kill him in cold blood. But then he couldn't be sure of that.

Mostly, he wondered what had caused her to do something this desperate—breaking into her father's office. Was this what she and Gage had been discussing in the alley? He noted that she'd put the ledger—if that indeed was what it was, into the canvas bag she carried, along with the flashlight.

They went back out the open window, with her right at his heels. "Where is your bike?" she whispered as she closed the window and locked the iron bars again, keeping the gun on him.

"My bike?" he asked stupidly. "You don't think you can handle a bike that size—"

"I just need to handle you," she interrupted. "You're getting us both out of here on that bike," she said, pressing the barrel of the weapon into his back as they moved through the shadows to the garage.

He wondered where she planned to take him as he climbed on the bike and she slid in behind him. Several possibilities crossed his mind. One involved a bullet to the back of the head and a ditch.

"Whatever you say, sweetheart."

"Don't call me sweetheart," she snapped.

"Whatever you say. But you'd better put this on if you hope to get out of here." He took the helmet from where he'd hooked it over the handlebar earlier. She snatched it out of his hand.

He could have taken her down right then fairly easily. After all, he was trained for this sort of thing. But he reminded himself that she believed he was nothing more than a chauffeur. Also, she needed him. There was no way she could handle the bike alone even if she did know how to ride and she apparently was desperate enough to take him with her. That meant he had her right where he wanted her. Kinda.

He punched the gas. She hurriedly wrapped one slim arm around him and held on, her body pressed tight to his. He felt her hand go up under his shirt until she found bare skin, her touch tantalizing torment. She pressed the cold barrel of the weapon against his ribs.

"Don't do anything stupid at the gate," she whispered next to his ear.

The guard at the gate didn't seem that surprised to see him come back through. The man was, however, surprised to see that Jesse had picked up a woman. Fortunately, the surprise gave Jesse just enough time to speed out of the gate before the guard could react.

"He's going to call your father," Jesse yelled back at Amanda.

She jabbed the gun into his side in answer. "Head south."

It would take only a few minutes for J.B. to verify that Amanda was gone before he sent his goons looking for her—and the chauffeur, who it appeared had helped her escape. Great.

Night lay over the city like a warm, wet blanket. In the distance, he saw the flicker of lightning but while he couldn't hear the rumble of the thunder over the roar of the bike, he could see that the storm was moving their way.

The air crackled with electricity but not all of it from the storm. He'd never felt her touch before. Except for that quick brush in the alley. Now her body clung to his, hotter than the Texas night. Her breasts crushed against his back, soft and rounded through her thin clothing; her spicy scent deadly. Amanda, armed and as always, dangerous.

His need made him ache; the wanting made him disgusted with himself. He knew who she was, what she was capable of, but the disgust seemed minor compared to the need. God, how he wanted her. And if he had the chance, he feared he'd take her. That scared him more than the gun in his ribs. Or the woman with her finger on the trigger.

She took him down a series of back roads outside of Dallas. He'd seen her checking her watch before they left the estate. She seemed anxious as if she had someplace she had to be.

He could feel her anxiety growing as if time were running out.

"Turn here," she ordered.

He recognized the neighborhood. It was just south of where she'd met the woman at the out-of-the-way Mexican café. Except this area was part of a city renewal program. The houses stood empty, windows broken out, graffiti scrawled on the weathered siding, waiting to be torn down. Almost all of the street lamps were out, and even what had once been a park stood empty, knee-deep in grass.

He felt his skin crawl, recalling his original fear: a ditch and a gunshot to the back of the head. *A fitting end for someone who'd started out in a ditch beside the road,* he thought bitterly.

"Stop the bike," Amanda ordered with another jab of the gun barrel.

He stopped, his patience wearing thin. And her desperation was starting to scare him a little.

"Get off," she ordered as she started to ease the gun from under his shirt. "Slowly."

He considered his options. He could let her kill him. He could let her leave him out here. Or...

He brought his arm down hard. She let out a cry. The weapon clattered to the concrete. In one swift movement, he jerked her off her feet and around onto his lap.

He'd had enough of her orders, enough of her. His body hurt from need, making him tense and irritable. Just being this close to her made him want to take her and get it over with. He knew it would be only the one time. He'd never want her again. He just needed to get her out of his system. Damn the consequences.

He stripped his bike helmet from her blond head and, trapping her arms, pulled her into him hard.

His mouth dropped to hers. He would have one kiss. One taste of her.

In the distance, he thought he heard thunder but in his fevered state of mind, it could just have easily been his own thunderous heart.

She fought for only a moment, then surrendered to his arms around her, his mouth on hers, his kiss. Her lips parted with a low moan and she softened against him.

Lightning lit the sky like fireworks. The answering thunder reverberated through him, making the night seem as alive as the rarified air around them.

And for a few moments, she was just a woman, not a mobster's daughter, but flesh and blood and more female than any woman he'd ever known. He freed her arms, deepening the kiss as she placed her palms on his chest.

Suddenly, she shoved him back. Before he could react, she snatched the cycle helmet from his hand and swung. He dodged. The helmet missed his head but glanced off his shoulder as he grabbed for her. But she'd already dropped the helmet, slid off the bike and was running toward the park.

His pride as well as his shoulder hurting, he went after her. Lightning splintered the sky. Thunder rumbled, closer this time.

He tackled her, throwing her down, landing with her under him in the cool, damp grass. She let out a grunt and a curse and fought beneath him. He held her down until she stopped resisting. He could hear her labored breathing but she didn't fight him as he rolled her over and looked down into her face.

In the faint light from one of the few remaining streetlights, he could see her hair fanned out over the dark-green grass, her face pale, her brown eyes wide. He leaned over her, his hands pressing her arms above her head, his body pinning hers to the ground.

She licked her lips and met his gaze, her eyes glittering with rage.

"What the hell is the deal with you?" he demanded, his head spinning from the kiss, from her behavior. For just a moment during the kiss, he'd thought she'd wanted him as much as he wanted her. Wrong. Obviously the kiss had only been a ruse for her. His aching shoulder could testify to that. He was just lucky it hadn't been his head.

"You have to let me go," she commanded through gritted teeth.

"So you can try to brain me again? Not likely."

"If my father finds out what you've done—"

"What *I've* done?" he interrupted. "Something tells me kissing you would be way down on the list long after breaking into his office. Try again."

She took a ragged breath. Tears glittered in her eyes. He could feel the fight go out of her.

"You don't understand," she whispered.

"Boy, you can say that again. Why don't you try to explain it to me." He had no idea what he didn't understand. Highest on his list would have been the kiss.

Over them, lightning lit the sky, thunder boomed as he held her down, determined to finally get some answers. One way or the other.

She looked up at him, her eyes swimming in tears. "Let me up and I'll tell you everything."

He really doubted that but she no longer seemed armed, although everything about Amanda he realized would always be dangerous. At least to him.

He let go of her arms. She lay still for a long moment. A voice inside his head warned him he was being played for the fool. Again. But he started to ease off her.

Suddenly she shot a furtive glance to her right. The canvas shoulder bag she'd been carrying was lying within her reach. She made a grab for it.

He'd seen her put the ledger and the flashlight in the bag, but he had no idea what else was in there. His mind screamed, *She's going for a weapon.*

He grabbed the strap of the bag before she could and tossed the bag just out of her reach.

The bag hit the edge of the sidewalk. Something inside shattered. The sound made him start as if it had been a gunshot.

She let out an oath and attacked him like a hell-cat. He fought to hold her down. What had been in the bag that would break and make her this upset?

"What was that?" he demanded as he braved releasing her with one hand to lean out and snag the bag. He dragged it back over to them; it left a wet trail in the grass.

She squirmed under him, cursing.

He frowned as he opened the bag to see what appeared to be a bottle of teething medicine. A pale liquid puddled in the bottom of the bag. No weapon.

His gaze flicked to hers in surprise.

She groaned, closed her eyes and lay still, no longer fighting. A tear squeezed from beneath her dark lashes. For a moment, he thought it might be a real tear with some emotion behind it. But then her eyes flew open and all he saw was anger.

"Get off me, you big oaf," she said through gritted teeth.

His head swam as he eased off her, but he still kept close enough that he could grab her again if it proved necessary.

But she made no move to take off or to attack. She knelt beside the bag in the grass, dumped out the pieces of the bottle, and carefully removed the ledger, checking to make sure the pages hadn't been ruined.

He watched her get to her feet and carefully turn the bag inside out and put the flashlight and the ledger inside again. "The medicine was for Susannah," he said, unable to hide his disgust. The woman was a liar. Her baby hadn't been kidnapped.

"What do you care about my baby?" she demanded angrily.

He opened his mouth, then closed it again. Why would a mobster's chauffeur care about the missing baby? "Maybe I could help you."

"Oh, sure, like you helped last night? Spying on me for my father?"

"J.B. had nothing to do with me following you last night," Jesse said, remembering too clearly the brush of Amanda's breast against his arm. Unconsciously, he rubbed the spot with his hand.

"Then how did he know about me going to the café?"

"Didn't you tell him about me following you?"

"I never told my father anything," she said flatly.

Jesse stared at her. She hadn't gone to her father. That shouldn't surprise him in light of everything else he'd learned about her tonight but it still did. It suddenly hit him. When J.B. had thanked him for keeping an eye on Amanda, he'd just been fishing. And Jesse had taken the bait.

"Gage told him about seeing the two of us together."

She blinked in surprise. "Gage?"

He nodded. "I overheard them."

Her jaw tightened. "What did Gage say?"

"That he was looking for Susannah."

She nodded as if she already knew that.

"You know it crossed my mind that you and Gage might have cooked this whole thing up to extort money from your father," he said, aware he was wading into dangerous waters. "Extortion does run in your family. But now I'm thinking J.B. didn't go for it. So you stole the ledger to give yourselves more leverage."

She shot him a look so deadly it should have killed him on the spot. "I can't stand Gage Ferraro and I don't want anything from my father."

Between her look and her tone, he tended to believe her. Her anger toward both men did make him curious, though.

"What is it you want from me?" she asked out of the blue. Her gaze searched his face, probing, intimate, disarming.

He swore silently at just the thought of what he really wanted from her as a man. As a cop, it was a whole different story. "I like you. I just—"

"You hate the sight of me," she corrected.

He took a breath. "I think you're rich and spoiled," he admitted, knowing he'd have to be as truthful as he dared. Amanda might be a lot of things, but she wasn't stupid.

"But...?" she asked, cocking her head to one side to study him.

The truth? "But I still want you."

Her lush mouth curved into a humorless smile, her eyes sultry and hotter than the Texas night. "You have a lot of nerve even saying something like that to me let alone kissing me without my permission. Do you have any idea what my father would do to you if he knew?"

"I have a pretty good notion."

"Doesn't that bother you?"

"Not as much as you bother me," he said, surprised at how honest he could be once he got started.

She shook her head and let out a low, sexy laugh. "You are one sure fool."

"Are you going to try to tell me you feel nothing?" he asked.

They stared at each other for a long moment, gazes locked. Lightning electrified the sky. Thunder boomed overhead. The first few drops of rain began to fall, hard and wet from the blackness.

"No," she said slowly, dragging her gaze away. "I feel contempt."

She glanced at her watch and let out a curse. Her gaze shot up to him. He watched her trying to decide what to do.

"Look," he said carefully. "It's obvious you need to be somewhere. Isn't that why you hijacked me and my bike? I'll take you there." He was afraid she'd changed her mind since hijacking him. Since he'd kissed her and acted like a fool.

Rain slashed downward in large, soaking drops.

For a moment she looked like she might cry again. This time though, he definitely wasn't going to buy it.

"What if I told you my life was in danger?" she asked.

Right. "Did you mention this to your father? I'm sure he has the manpower to do something about it." If it were even remotely true.

"He might have ordered the hit," she said, seemingly oblivious to the rain that now soaked them to their skin.

He frowned, getting real tired of her lies. "Your father adores you and wouldn't touch a hair on your head. At least he did before you broke into his office and took—" he waved a hand at the bag she now clutched to her chest "—whatever is in that book." What *was* in that ledger?

"You think this is a game," she said shoving her wet hair back from her face as she glared up at him.

"I think you're playing with me, yes."

She raised one fine brow in answer. He saw her shiver and look again at her watch, the dial lighting up for an instant in the dark and rain. ''There isn't time to talk about this now.''

She turned and strode in the direction of the bike. She was back on her high horse.

He watched her strut her stuff, head high, princess of the palace, swinging that cute little behind as she just walked away from him toward the bike as if she'd never held him at gunpoint, or broken into her father's office, or kissed him with a passion like she meant it or tried to coldcock him with a bike helmet. This was probably just another run-of-the-mill day for a woman like her.

He swore and followed her, frustrated in more ways than he wanted to count. Where was she taking him? He could only hope it was to Susannah. Spending time around this woman was pure torture. And he sensed she was enjoying putting him through it.

He also knew going with her would be dangerous. Being within a mile of her was dangerous. Gage and his goons could be waiting for them. J.B. could already know about the missing ledger. Just about anything could be waiting for them.

But wherever she had to be was important. Important enough that she was now willing, although reluctantly, to let him take her. He tried to look at it as a victory of sorts.

The rain fell, hard and wet and unrelenting. The

sky over the city crackled with light. Thunder rumbled as it moved off.

Closer he heard a car engine. At first just a low throbbing pulse. He glanced up the empty street. No lights. But the car was close, the engine had a distinct knock to it.

His heart took off at a sprint. They'd been followed.

"Amanda!"

She didn't turn, just kept walking through the rain as if she hadn't heard him. She scooped up the helmet from the grass and started across the street toward his motorcycle.

"Amanda!"

The car came out from behind one of the deserted buildings just on the other side of Amanda. It headed right for her, tires screeching on the wet pavement.

Chapter Six

Amanda heard the car too late. She turned, instantly blinded by the sudden flash of headlights and the realization that the car intended to run her down.

Before she could react, Jesse slammed into her, driving her from the street. They landed in the weeds at the edge of the pavement. The car sped past, so close she heard the crunch of tires next to her and felt the breeze it made as it passed.

"Are you all right?"

She lay in the dirt, too shocked to move.

"Amanda?"

"Yes?"

"We have to get out of here," he said, his voice seeming far away. "They might come back."

She let him help her to her feet. As she glanced after the speeding car, a quiet despair filled her. If she had any doubts about how much trouble she was in, she didn't anymore.

"Come on." Jesse half dragged her to his bike. "We have to get out of here," he repeated urgently.

She glanced down the street. No car lights. No sound of an engine. "They won't be back," she said. "It was just a warning. My father only wanted to scare me. This time."

Jesse stopped walking abruptly and spun around to face her. "You're not going to tell me *that* was your father's doing?"

She wasn't going to tell him anything. She stepped around him, feeling coming back into her limbs, back into her numb mind. She walked toward the bike. He worked for her father. Surely he knew the kind of man J. B. Crowe was.

"You could have been killed!" Jesse called after her.

She hadn't expected things to escalate this quickly, this radically, but she should have. How far would her father go? That's what frightened her most now.

She heard Jesse behind her.

"Even if your father found out about the break-in and that the ledger was missing—"

"Believe me, if my father already knew, that car would not have missed."

He stared at her, disbelieving, and she wondered again if he had no idea what kind of man he worked for. Surely...

"If this isn't about the ledger, then…this is about Susannah, isn't it?" he said, drawing in a breath.

She felt her heart jump inside her chest as she looked at him. "I thought you said we had to get out of here?"

"Listen to me," he said grabbing her shoulders and turning her to face him. "Whatever is going on, it isn't just your life and Susannah's you're jeopardizing but also Diana Kincaid's."

She frowned in confusion. "The governor's daughter? What does she have to do with me or my father?"

"Don't tell me you're that naive." He released her as if touching her repulsed him. "Your father thinks Governor Kincaid is behind Susannah's kidnapping. Did you really think he wouldn't retaliate? Especially since Diana Kincaid is pregnant."

Her legs suddenly felt boneless. She leaned against the bike for support. There was a time when she would have argued vehemently in her father's defense. Now it would have been a waste of breath. She knew better than anyone what her father was capable of. This news just confirmed her worst fears.

But what about Jesse, she thought, studying him in the dim light of the solitary street lamp. How did he know Diana Kincaid had been taken? As far as she knew, it hadn't been on the ncws. "What does J. B. Crowe's chauffeur care about the governor's daughter?'' she asked, her heart in her throat.

"Maybe I just don't like to see innocent people hurt," he said. "Anyway, I would think the two of you have a lot in common. Daughters of powerful fathers. Both young women with a baby or one on the way, and no husband."

Both being used as pawns.

"Both afraid." He reached out to touch her cheek, his look filled with compassion.

She stepped back, afraid that if she let him get too close, if she let him comfort her, she would break down. The thought of finding comfort in his arms was much too appealing. All the pain and anger and fear would come out in a rush of tears and she would bury her face in his shoulder and, in his arms, tell him everything in her need to confide in someone the awful truth.

But forgetting he worked for her father, forgetting that this man had followed her last night, wasn't something she was apt to do.

"The difference is," she said drawing on her anger to give her strength, "Diana still has *her* baby."

"If you tell the truth before it's too late—"

"It's already too late," she snapped. "I can't help Diana Kincaid. Isn't it obvious I can't even protect *myself* from my father? Now are you going to take me where I have to go or not?''

"Let's go.''

HE FOLLOWED her to the motorcycle, chilled by the coldness he'd heard in her voice. Coldness and anger and hurt. Was it possible she was as much a victim as Diana Kincaid?

"Just a minute.''

She turned to frown over her shoulder at him.

He held out his hand. "Give it to me.''

Surprise and innocence flickered in her eyes.

"The gun,'' he said, still holding out his hand. The one that had clattered to the concrete beneath his motorcycle when he'd disarmed her. He wasn't sure when she'd picked it up without him seeing her do it. But he was damned sure she had.

With obvious reluctance, she reached up under her jacket and fished the pistol out of the waistband of her jeans and handed it to him.

He stuck it in his own jeans. "Now the ledger.''

Her eyes glittered in the dim light with anger and she stepped back as if he'd slapped her.

"Just until I find out what's going on,'' he said.

For a moment, he thought she would fight him on this. To his surprise, she handed him the ledger without a word. He couldn't shake off the worry that she'd given in way too easily. He desperately wanted to open the book and see what was so important that she would risk everything to get it. But it was too dark and she seemed in a hurry, so he stuffed it in his jacket pocket.

He swung onto the bike, wondering why she hadn't used the gun against him when she'd had the chance.

She climbed on behind him, still silent, and circled his waist with her arms, pressing her face and body against his back as if needing his warmth, his strength. He sensed a vulnerability in her that gave him a twinge of guilt.

If Amanda had kidnapped Susannah with Gage's help as Jesse believed she had, then Jesse would have to arrest her when the time came. What bothered him as he started the bike was that when he did, he'd be throwing her to the wolves. A cold dread filled him at the thought of what J. B. Crowe would do when he found out everything his precious daughter had done.

"Where to?" he asked over his shoulder.

SHE TOOK HIM straight to a house not far down the road. In the motorcycle's headlight, he could see that the place was old, isolated and in need of a lot more than paint, though paint would have helped. He could only assume after seeing the teething medicine in her bag that she was taking him to Susannah. It seemed an odd place for

Amanda to have left her baby based on her father's net worth.

"This is it?" Jesse asked shining the cycle's headlight at the groves of trees off three sides of the house. It appeared to be a pecan orchard.

No lights burned inside the house. Nor was there a vehicle around. For not the first time, he wondered if she'd led him into a trap. Or another wild-goose chase.

She swung off the bike and started for the house.

"Hold on a minute."

She turned, her look impatient, wary. She no longer seemed vulnerable and now he wondered if she ever had been or he'd just imagined it.

He killed the motor, stood the bike on its kick-stand and swung off, keeping his eye on her.

She'd stopped at the foot of the dilapidated steps. She watched him walk toward her, her ex-pression worried as she glanced out into the night, as if looking for the dark car.

He slowed at the sound of a baby crying softly and something beyond that sound. The soft mur-mur of a woman's voice trying to still the infant.

He glanced at Amanda. She seemed anxious to get into the house. And nervous.

He looked over his shoulder, also half expecting to see that same dark car parked up the road, motor idling. He recalled the knock of the engine.

But there was no car idling nearby, no distinct

knock of the engine, no sound at all. The road was empty this far out of town, this late at night and he was pretty sure they hadn't been followed. Then again, he'd been pretty sure before and look what had happened. But unlike Amanda, he didn't think J. B. Crowe was behind it.

They climbed the steps to the wide, worn wooden porch. Amanda rushed ahead to knock on the front door. He heard footfalls inside. The porch light came on. The faded curtains at the window parted. The lock thunked and the door opened.

The woman standing framed in the door was younger than Amanda with black hair and obviously of Mexican heritage.

"Buenas noches," she said to Amanda, then looked at Jesse with concern.

Amanda kissed the woman's cheek and rattled off something in Spanish, most of which Jesse didn't catch. His Spanish was passable at best. Obviously Amanda was fluent.

"English, please," he said catching hold of Amanda's arm.

"This is my friend, Carina." She wiggled out of his hold. "This is my father's chauffeur, Jesse."

He didn't miss the way she'd put him in his place, reminding them all who he worked for.

"The baby has been fussy all night," Carina said and looked hopefully at Amanda.

Amanda shook her head. "It was broken." She shot Jesse an accusing look.

"It will be fine," Carina said. "I was just heating a bottle." She headed toward the kitchen.

The house was small inside. Just the one floor and he could see all of the rooms with the doors standing open. From inside one of the rooms, a baby began to cry again.

He moved toward the bedroom, following the sound, eager to see Susannah.

He heard Amanda right behind him as he entered the small bedroom. A single baby carrier sat beside a narrow unmade twin bed. He moved to it and the sound of the crying baby, expectation making his legs strangely weak.

The baby was beautiful, her skin a rich, warm bronze, eyes dark and wide and filled with tears.

"This isn't Susannah," he said in disbelief as Amanda pushed him out of the way and picked up the baby. The infant quit crying instantly. There was no other carrier in the room, no other baby.

"Of course it isn't Susannah," Amanda said tersely. "Susannah's been kidnapped."

He looked around the room, wondering why she'd brought him here. This couldn't be why she'd been in such a rush. Not to deliver teething medicine to this baby.

He looked at her. Her hair was wet and dark against her lightly suntanned skin. Her eyes were wide and golden. She looked young and scared and surprisingly innocent. And holding another woman's baby with such obvious love and compassion.

"I know you're in trouble," he said quietly. "I can help you."

"Yeah, so far, you've been an incredible help," she said sarcastically, as the baby in her arms began to fuss, its little mouth opening and closing like a bird's.

Short of admitting he was a cop working undercover, he didn't know how to convince her to trust him.

He stared at her as she rocked the baby in her arms and cooed softly to it. He wanted to shake her until her teeth rattled. But the anger dissipated in an instant at the heart-wrenching look on her face as she gazed down at the other woman's child. The suffering he witnessed in her expression made him doubt everything he had believed about this woman and left him stunned. She wasn't the heartless, unfeeling woman he'd wanted to believe she was. She wouldn't have harmed her own baby. Not this woman.

He thought of her desperation, of the gum medicine she'd brought the baby, of the car that had tried to run her down. Dear God. What was Amanda Crowe running from? The answer seemed all too obvious. Her father.

Jesse could believe she had someone to fear. He just didn't believe it was J. B. Crowe.

Her gaze raised to his and the pain he saw almost leveled him. He stood looking at her, shaken. The cop in him reminded him that Susannah was still missing. And until she was found, another mother and her child were in jeopardy. All of this had to be stopped before J. B. Crowe retaliated further. But the man in him could only wonder what had happened to bring Amanda to this point in her life.

Carina came into the room with the bottle of milk.

"You have a beautiful baby," he managed to say.

Carina gave him a worried smile. Whatever was going on, she knew, he realized.

Amanda seemed reluctant to give up the infant, but slowly handed the baby to Carina who offered the bottle of formula. The baby sucked greedily and Jesse felt a pull inside him, an ache that he couldn't put a name to.

"We have to go," Amanda said checking her watch again. She added something in Spanish.

Carina frowned and looked worried, then kissed Amanda's cheek, hugged her and thanked her. *"Vaya con Dios."*

"What did you say to her?" Jesse asked as they headed for the front door.

"I told her I wouldn't be able to visit for a while," she said.

"Oh?"

She stopped at the door, turning unexpectedly. He saw the gun in her hand and swore. Carina must have slipped it to her when they'd hugged.

"Give me the ledger," she said quietly.

He shook his head. "I can't let you do this."

"You can't stop me, Jesse. I need the ledger. Now."

Outside, he heard a sound like the creak of a porch floorboard.

"You don't want to go out there alone," he said, every instinct telling him it was true.

"I need the ledger to trade for my baby," she said, her voice almost a whisper. "Don't make me shoot you for it."

"You're making a mistake," he said, but he pulled the ledger from his pocket. For some reason he believed she was desperate enough to pull the trigger. He'd already witnessed the extremes she'd gone to to get the ledger.

He held it out. When she reached for it, he jerked it back with one hand and grabbed the gun with the other, twisting the weapon from her fingers.

"Now," he said, his voice as low as hers had been, "we're going out there together and face the kidnappers."

"You're the one who's making the mistake now," she said angrily. "You don't have any idea what you're getting involved in."

"I appreciate your concern," he said sarcastically. He could feel her gaze boring into him.

"Who are you?" she asked. "You aren't a chauffeur."

"Not anymore." Holding the gun out of sight, he opened the door and listened. Silence answered him and for a moment, he thought he might have been wrong about a lot of things.

Then he caught movement out of the corner of his eye at the edge of the porch railing.

Instinctively, he grabbed Amanda as he raised the gun, already pulling her back.

A set of headlights flashed on. "Police!"

Chapter Seven

Jesse swore as he pulled Amanda back into the house, slammed the door and locked it behind them.

"You bastard," Amanda spat and tried to squirm out of his grip. "I knew I couldn't trust you."

So had this been some sort of test? "This sure as hell isn't my doing, sweetheart," he said as he snapped off the porch light and pulled her over against the wall beside the door. "Tell Carina to turn out the other lights, get the baby and stay down."

But the moment he said it, he realized the lights were already out and Carina and the baby were gone. In the distance he heard the sound of an engine dying away in the darkness. Out front one of the cops was calling for them to come out with their hands up. He tried to tell himself that the cops had made a mistake.

But he knew better. Amanda had been set up. Or he had.

"What are you trying to pull?" he demanded, tightening his hold on her. Her body felt hot to the touch. Soft, supple and full, yet strong. A body that held more secrets than he cared to contemplate.

"What am I trying to pull? You don't think *I* called the cops?" she snapped.

"Well, you *know* I didn't call them. What about your friend, how did she know to hightail so fast?" he demanded.

"She's an illegal. She's always ready to take off at a moment's notice. She must have heard the police and thought they were after *her*."

He considered that, wondering if Amanda might be telling the truth this time. He doubted it. At least not in its entirety. "That story about trading the ledger for Susannah—"

"That wasn't a story," she snapped.

"Look, *someone* called the cops."

"Or maybe you have some sort of tracking device on your bike."

"Yeah, right, just in case I'm ever hijacked at gunpoint." He didn't tell her that he rode a bike for that very reason. Easy to sweep and something he did regularly. He liked to know if he was being tracked.

She swore. "Or the kidnapper set me up," she said angrily.

Now would probably be a good time to tell her he was an undercover cop. And tell the guys outside as well. A thought struck him. He groaned. ''Any chance your father has someone on the force in his pocket?''

In the light filtering in from the cop car's headlights outside, she gave him a look that said even he couldn't be *that* stupid. ''My father's never had so much as a parking ticket in the city of Dallas since he took over as the head of the Organization. Does that answer your question?''

''Great.'' He wasn't sure what bothered him most—her nonchalant view of her father's life of crime or the fact that some of Jesse's brothers in blue were on J.B.'s payroll. ''Do you know which cops are on your father's payroll?''

''Don't you?'' she asked.

So now she thought he was a dirty cop. Things just kept getting better.

He parted the curtains and looked out. He could see one of the officers outside on the porch. The same one he'd caught sight of moments before. Sergeant Brice Olsen. A cop from another division he knew and who knew him.

There appeared to be just one other officer out front. Possibly another one or two out back. Not exactly a large raid and he couldn't hear any backup on its way. At least not yet. Was it possible Brice was on J.B.'s payroll? Or did this raid have something to do with Diana Kincaid's disappearance?

Jesse figured he and Amanda could have been followed. After all, she'd almost been run down not far from here. But it seemed doubtful. More than likely someone had known exactly where Amanda was going to be.

Not that it mattered now. If Brice was legit, then Jesse knew he could clear this up in a matter of minutes—if he wanted to blow his cover. But if Brice worked for J. B. Crowe, or worse, a competing mobster like Mickie Ferraro—

Outside the cop hollered for them to come out on the count of ten or they were coming in.

"They can't get their hands on this ledger," Amanda said, desperation in her voice.

"The ledger. Yeah, forget the fact that they might kill us," he said, unable to hold back the sarcasm.

"If they get this ledger, my baby will die," she snapped and jerked free of him. "There is only one thing to do. You're going to have to take me hostage."

He stared down at her. "You have to be kidding. Do you realize how dangerous—"

"At this point, getting shot by dirty cops is the least of my worries," she snarled. "Put the gun to my head and you'd damned well better be convincing or we are both dead."

Outside the cop was nearing the number ten.
Jesse swore. "No way."

"Or I could take you hostage," she suggested.

At least the woman had a sense of humor.

Jesse swore again and called out, "We're coming out! Don't shoot!" He looked at Amanda. "And if this doesn't work?"

"Then you'll just have to shoot me," she said.

"Don't tempt me," he growled into her ear as he pulled her to him.

He pressed the end of the barrel snugly against her chin until she raised her head and was forced to look up at him as she leaned against him.

"Ready?" he enquired. His traitorous body didn't have the good sense not to react to the feel of her compact behind pressed against his thighs.

"Not as ready as you, it seems," she said lightly.

Outside the cop yelled again for them to come out.

"Look," she said sounding dead serious again. "There's a car hidden out in the pecan trees off to the left of the house."

His first instinct was not to believe her. "How do you know that?"

"I hid it there."

He tried to imagine what she had to gain by lying, but he suspected lying came as naturally to her as breathing. "Where are the keys?"

"On the top of the front right tire."

He hesitated, but only for a moment. Outside one of the cops yelled for them to come out now. At this point, he had little choice.

"We're coming out!" He opened the door a crack, using Amanda as a shield. It had to be the riskiest, craziest thing he'd ever done. But she was right. There didn't seem to be any other way. No cop, clean or dirty, was going to shoot a woman down in cold blood. Especially the daughter of mobster J. B. Crowe. At least he hoped not.

He shoved Amanda through the door in front of him, hoping he was right about her being the key to getting them out of there alive.

"Cut the lights!" he yelled once he was sure they'd seen his hostage.

The headlights blinked off. It took a moment for his eyes to adjust. "Don't shoot!" He moved them slowly out onto the porch as he looked for a sniper.

The storm had passed, leaving the sky scrubbed clean. Stars glittered brightly. The moon lit the pecan trees ringing the house and the stretch of dried yard in front.

He could see there were three cops; Brice was the only one he recognized. He could also see that this wasn't a standard raid. "Drop your weapons and move back or I'll kill her," he ordered.

Brice saw him and a look passed between them in the moonlight. The cop dropped his weapon first. "Do as he says," he ordered the others. Reluctantly, they dropped their guns and moved back.

Jesse worked his way with Amanda in front of him toward the pecan trees off to his left where she said the car would be waiting for them. He hoped she was telling the truth. His motorcycle lay on its side, obviously disabled. The only other option was taking the cop car he saw parked up the road—a little too conspicuous a ride.

"Don't follow us and no harm will come to the woman," he said, realizing he sounded like a late-night B-movie villain.

"Let him go!" Brice said, sounding dubious. It was obvious Brice wasn't sure what Jesse was up to or which side he was on, but the cop was going to go along with it.

The other two cops didn't seem happy about the turn of events, but they didn't move as Jesse dragged Amanda farther back into the trees.

Just to make sure Brice and his buddies didn't change their minds, Jesse fired a couple of shots into the two front tires of their police car.

"Now!" he cried to Amanda and grabbing her hand, ran.

Amazingly, the getaway car was just where she said it would be. A minivan, a nondescript tan, the keys on the right front tire. He took the keys, opened the passenger side door and pushed her over behind the wheel as he followed her inside.

"Drive!" he ordered, handing her the keys.

The van engine turned over on the first try. She swung the van around and headed in the opposite direction of the house as if she knew where she was going.

He quickly glanced over his shoulder into the back, afraid he'd walked into another trap. The rear of the van was filled with a half dozen suitcases and an assortment of cardboard boxes.

Out the rear window, he could see nothing but darkness. He didn't think Brice would come after them. At least not until the cop checked with his superior. If that was J. B. Crowe, then it would be just a matter of time before Jesse saw the cop again.

Amanda took off through the pecan trees along a dirt track, sans headlights, following the pale silver path of moonlight between the limbs.

As soon as he was sure they weren't being followed, he reached back and pulled a carry-on flight bag to him. What he found inside wasn't much of a surprise. Baby clothes. And tucked in the side of the bag, plane tickets and a passport. He opened the passport in the light from the dash and saw that it was for Elizabeth Greenough.

He glanced over at her, but she didn't look at him as he put everything back where he'd found it and sat holding the weapon in his hand, trying to decide what to do now.

"You can put the gun away," she said as they bounced along beneath the dark branches of the pecan trees. "I don't want to be caught by those men any more than you do. And you aren't going to shoot me."

There were moments he might have argued that. This wasn't one of them. He now had both of Amanda's weapons. He checked the clip on each, then slipped one gun into the waist of his jeans and the other into the glove box.

He glanced over at Amanda as she swung the van onto a narrow tree-lined dirt road. The limbs of the trees scraped the top of the van as she drove. Through the leaves he caught glimpses of the full moon.

He studied her, trying to put all the pieces together, all the different Amandas he'd witnessed over the last two weeks. She was a mystery to him. One he desperately needed to solve if he hoped to keep them both alive.

The problem was, he didn't know what to believe. Back at the house she'd convinced him that her baby had been kidnapped. Now he couldn't even be sure the hit-and-run hadn't been staged for his benefit and maybe even the raid on the house back there. He couldn't be sure of anything. Not with this woman. And yet he sensed he'd only run into the tip of the iceberg. Either way, his ship was sinking.

He'd blown his assignment. He was no longer working undercover to try to bring down J. B. Crowe and his empire. Now he was on the run with Crowe's daughter. If that didn't get him killed he didn't know what would.

On top of that he didn't know where Susannah was, who had her, if she'd really been kidnapped or not. And now his cover was blown with J.B. even if the mobster didn't find out he was a cop. To make matters worse, both his life and Amanda's were on the line and he didn't even know for sure who they had to fear.

He glanced back. No sign in the moonlight of another vehicle following. Nothing but the moonlit darkness.

Amanda had driven down a series of narrow, dirt roads until even the distant sky no longer glowed with the lights of Dallas. She drove with more skill than he would have guessed, but no less self-assurance. The woman was gutsy, he'd give her that.

He glanced over at her again as she wheeled the van down the dirt road, the moon flickering through the trees, the sweet hot Texas air blowing in through the vents.

His heart picked up a beat as he realized how alone they were in this isolated place, how impossibly alluring she was even now, still wet from the rain, still as deceptive and devious as ever.

Her T-shirt hugged her full curves, molding her breasts, the hard buds of her nipples pushing against the cloth. He could almost taste them. He breathed in her scent—a combination of wet and warm—and let out a tortured breath.

"Pull over."

Chapter Eight

Amanda glanced at the empty stretch of dirt road ahead. No cars. No houses. Just the limbs of the trees etched black against the night sky, leaves dark and restless in the breeze. She felt a sliver of fear as she reminded herself that she didn't really know this man or what he was capable of. She'd already misjudged him on several occasions. Misjudging him now could prove fatal.

"Pull over," he repeated, his voice deadly quiet.

She slowed the van to a stop. He reached over, and for a moment, she thought he was going to touch her. He turned off the lights, the engine. Darkness and silence settled around them, wrapping them in its humid cloak.

She had thought Jesse was nothing more than her father's chauffeur. She had thought she could handle him. Neither, it seemed, was the case.

She inched her left hand to the door handle. The metal felt cool to the touch.

''We have a problem,'' Jesse said in that same quiet voice.

He didn't know how much of a problem they had, she thought. She said nothing, waiting, heart hammering as she measured her chances of getting the door open and throwing herself out before he could grab her. Not good. Especially since she needed the ledger—and he had it.

''I'm not a crooked cop,'' he said softly. ''I'm not on your father's payroll. Not even as a chauffeur as of tonight.''

''Why should I care?'' she asked, trying to adopt a nonchalance she didn't feel.

''But I *am* a cop.''

She dropped her gaze. She didn't dare look at him. He thought being a cop would relieve her mind? That that would make her trust him? Confide her deepest secrets to him?

She wanted to laugh. And cry. A cop. She swallowed, feeling sick to her stomach. One of her earliest memories was of the police coming to the door late at night and dragging her father out while she and her mother cried and tried to fight them off. One cop called her names, meaningless words to her at that age and yet she had understood perfectly what the man had thought of her and her family. Cops had always been the enemy. Even the ones her father now could afford to buy.

''I've been working —''

"I don't care who you are," she interrupted quickly. She didn't want to hear it.

"I don't want you thinking I'm one of your father's dirty cops."

Something in his voice made her look over at him. The moonlight captured his features, giving her a jolt. Sometimes she forgot how dangerous he looked. Or how handsome, which made him all the more dangerous.

"I told you, I don't care," she said.

"Doesn't it make any difference that I'm a cop?"

She let out a groan. "Oh, yeah. I trust you even less than when you were just my father's chauffeur."

He shook his head. "I can't win for losing with you, can I?" His look was full of hunger. It made her skin warm from its heat. Made her body ache just seeing the desire in his eyes. He wanted her. Maybe more than he wanted the truth.

But it would be a cold day in Texas before he'd have her. She knew that was her only weapon against him. His desire.

And her greatest weakness. Her own.

He was a cop. The enemy. And cop or not, as long as he had the ledger she would have to handle him very carefully. The problem was, now she also knew that he wasn't going to just give her the ledger and let her go. And that was going to be a problem.

JESSE BLAMED the heat, his growing frustrations and the intimacy of the moonlight and pockets of darkness inside the van. "I need the truth." He needed a lot more than that. He needed her and that shook him to his very foundation.

She was the daughter of a mobster, involved in who only knew what and as far as he could tell up to her pretty little neck in deep doo. And now she'd pulled him in with her. And all he could think about was taking her in his arms and ending whatever this was between them, this desire that demanded satisfaction, this terrible ache that clouded his thinking.

What was it about this woman? Any fool could see behind that wide-eyed, injured innocence of hers. Why her?

"You already know the truth," she said, an edge to her voice. "What are you so afraid of? That you might be wrong about me? Or that you might be right? Worse, that it doesn't matter either way?"

He shook his head, angry with her, angry with himself. What she said was true. Worse, she'd seen his futile struggle to resist her. They both knew she was a deadly temptation. The problem was, he'd always believed himself above such captivation.

"The only truth I know is that you're a thief and a liar," he returned, wanting to hurt her, wanting to push her as far away as he could.

She brought up her hand to slap him but he caught it before her palm reached its mark.

He jerked her to him and groaned as he dropped his mouth to hers, his kiss punishing. She seemed small in his arms. Small and vulnerable. She put up no resistance. Made no sound. Her resignation proving to them both how right she was about him.

He shoved her back, despising himself for wanting her and despising her for having this power over him. His palm felt burned where her hand had been, he could taste her on his lips and her scent infused his senses as permanently as a brand. Somehow he'd let this woman get under his skin. And she would get him killed if he didn't get her out.

"Those suitcases back there, Susannah's clothes, the passport, the airline tickets for the two of you, they're all proof that you're a liar."

She brushed her fingers slowly over her bruised lips, tears welling in her eyes. "I know I'm a lot of things you abhor, Mr. Brock, but even I wouldn't lie about my daughter being kidnapped," she said, her voice dangerously soft. "Or is Brock even your real name? Who is the liar here?" Her eyes fired with anger. "Would you even recognize the truth if you heard it?"

"Try me," he challenged. "Let's hear some truth from those lips of yours."

She glared at him for a long moment, then took a breath. "The day my daughter Susannah was kidnapped, I got a call from Gage Ferraro. He told me he'd been contacted by the kidnappers and that they had demanded a ransom for our daughter."

"The kidnappers went to Ferraro instead of your father?" he asked, already having trouble believing her story. Gage was small potatoes. If they wanted any large amount of money they'd go to J.B. But they didn't want money, did they? "They demanded evidence against your father."

She nodded. "I was to make the trade tonight. But when the police showed up..."

He heard the pain in her voice. Was it possible she hadn't kidnapped her own daughter, hadn't been working with Gage, that she was telling the truth for once?

He pulled out the ledger he'd taken from her and opened it. He shot her a look, his heart pounding. He recognized the handwriting. J. B. Crowe had left him several messages during the time he'd worked as the mobster's chauffeur, all in a small, neat, very vertical, very distinctive script.

And even in the dim light from the dash and the moonlight filtering in through the windows, he could see that the pages were filled with numbers and dates. "Is this what I think it is?"

She nodded. "An account of my father's illegal activities. Enough to send him to prison."

Jesse let out a low whistle. "You planned to trade this for Susannah."

The look in her eyes told him how painful that decision had been. She'd betrayed her father to save her daughter. He no longer doubted that Susannah really had been kidnapped.

HE LOOKED AGAIN at the book, realizing just what he held in his hands. Something that could bring down J. B. Crowe and his empire.

Amanda touched his arm as if she could see what he desperately wanted to do with the evidence against her father. "If you turn that over to the police, it will be a death sentence for Diana Kincaid and her baby as well as mine."

"It would stop your father," he said.

"Do you really believe that putting him behind bars will stop him?" She shook her head. "The kidnapper will kill my daughter if he doesn't get that ledger. And believe me, my father will see that the same thing happens to Diana and her child."

Jesse swore. She was right. This was a helluva lot more complicated that he'd first imagined. He looked down the road and realized they'd been sitting still too long.

But he didn't know where to go. Or what to do.

Crowe would be looking for them. And the cops and the kidnapper. And God only knew who else.

"Tell me about the trade," he said.

"The kidnapper was to bring Susannah to the house and we would make the trade there," she said.

"Whose idea was that?"

"Mine," she said. "I wanted some control. My father owns the place. I knew Carina would be there and could get some things ready, like the car and the items I needed for after the trade."

"You trust this woman?" he asked, recalling how the police had suddenly appeared—and Carina had disappeared.

"Carina is one of the few people I do trust," she said flatly.

"What about your father?" Jesse had to ask. "If you had gone to him about this—"

She shook her head adamantly, reinforcing the sense that something had happened between Amanda and her father. "My father is a mobster."

He looked at her to see if she was serious. "You make it sound as if you just found out what your father does for a living."

Her look was lethal parts anger and hurt. "I've known he was a mobster since I was a kid. But I didn't know about some of his...activities until I started looking for evidence to trade for my daughter."

Jesse held his breath. "What did you find?"

"My father is running a black market baby ring," she said quietly. "He buys some babies, steals others from their mothers, and sells them to the highest bidder." Her voice reeked with contempt.

"How do you know this?" he asked. "Is this in the ledger?"

She shook her head. "Carina worked at the estate until about four months ago, when she had her baby," she said. "My father's men tried to buy her baby. They put pressure on her since she has no husband and she's an illegal immigrant. When she refused to give up her daughter, they tried to steal her." Amanda's gaze settled on his. "They tried to kill Carina. I just found out about it."

Jesse didn't know what to say.

"Now do you understand why, once I get my daughter, I'm leaving the country?" she asked. "I have to. To my father, family is everything because our blood binds us together, family is ownership," she said. "Susannah's curse is that Crowe blood runs through her veins. For that we are all going to suffer because my father will not rest until he has what he considers his."

Jesse wondered what blood ran through his own veins. And what curse it would bring with it. "What happens now?"

"I contact Gage and have him set up another trade."

"You trust him?"

She shot Jesse a look. "Only as far as I can throw him. But he's more upset over Susannah's kidnapping than I would have ever expected. I'd never seen him like that. Scared. He was practically in tears when he came to me about the trade, afraid I couldn't do what had to be done."

He heard the sorrow and pain in her voice, understood for the first time how hard this had been on her and just what extremes she would go to to save her daughter. The brave front she'd put on after the kidnapping had made him think she was lying. Now he realized acting tough was all that had kept her going—being strong, doing what needed to be done, keeping it together—until she could get her daughter back.

"You seem confident the kidnapper will agree to another trade," he said.   She nodded. "He wants that ledger. I need to call Gage and set it up."

Jesse nodded. "But how do you know the kidnapper—or Gage—didn't set you up back there?"

"I don't. But I still have the ledger and I know how badly the kidnapper wants it. He'll set up another trade."

That's what Jesse was worried about. Another trade. Another trap.

She pulled a cell phone from the compartment between the seats.

He watched her tap out a number and hoped to hell he wasn't making another mistake with this woman. She could be calling anyone.

"I want to hear what's being said," he told her.

She looked over at him, seemingly amused by his continued lack of trust. "You really are a cop, aren't you?" She leaned toward Jesse, tilting the phone so he could hear the conversation. "Gage?"

"Where the hell are you?" Gage demanded. Amanda was right, he sounded panicked.

"The trade didn't go down," she said. "But I would imagine you already know that."

"You're telling me? I got a call from the pickup person. He's furious. He saw the cops and took off. He thinks you pulled a fast one. What the hell went wrong?"

"You tell me," she said.

Gage let out a nervous laugh. "Yeah, right. *I* called the cops. Not even you believe that. You must have been followed. Probably your old man. I thought you said you'd be careful."

She glanced over at Jesse. "I'm doing my best." She sounded close to tears. He almost felt sorry for her.

Gage swore. "But you still have the ledger?"

"Yes, I want you to set up another trade."

Gage let out another oath. "Let me handle it this time."

"No, I make the trade, that's the deal."

It was obvious that Gage didn't like that. Jesse could hear him slamming things around on the other end of the line.

"It's going to take time," he said finally, sounding angry, frustrated. "A day or two at least. The kidnapper is demanding his own site this time. He's suspicious now. Where are you so I can let you know?"

"I'll contact you tomorrow," she said and clicked off.

Jesse stared out the windshield, unable to shake off the ominous feeling that had settled over him.

The moonlight paved a silver path between the trees and down the long narrow dirt road. The night air drifted in through their open windows, muggy and hot. He could smell something rotting in the trees.

"You act like you know who the kidnapper is," he said.

She didn't answer.

He looked over at her. She had her head down and he realized she was crying softly. It surprised him because for the first time he didn't think the tears were for his benefit.

Her short blond hair was spun silver in the moonlight. She raised her face slowly. The light

turned the tears on her cheeks to sparkling dia-
monds. She brushed them away with her hand,
seemingly embarrassed to be crying real tears.

Her gaze locked with his, challenging in its intensity. ''Governor Kincaid had my daughter kidnapped.''

Chapter Nine

She expected him to call her a liar again. She expected him to at least argue with her. The last thing she expected was him to say, "I'll drive."

"Wait a minute, where are we going?" She didn't like the look in his eyes.

"Red River, Texas," he said and motioned for her to switch seats with him. "I have some business there and we have at least a day before the next trade."

"What about the ledger?" she demanded as she reluctantly relinquished the driver's seat. She didn't give a damn about his other business. "You aren't going to keep me from making the trade."

"I'm not about to stop the trade," Jesse said without looking at her as he started the van. "Gage said it would be at least one day, maybe two. Red River is only a few hours' drive from here. We can be back in plenty of time. And obviously we can't stay in Dallas. No one will be looking for us in Red River.''

His argument made sense. ''Then you promise to give me the ledger when I need it and stay out of my way?'' she persisted, wondering why she thought she could trust him even if he did agree to her terms. As if she were in any position to be laying down terms.

''I told you,'' he said as he drove. ''I'm a cop. I want the kidnapper as much as you do.''

''I could care less about the kidnapper,'' she snapped. ''I just want my daughter.''

He looked over at her as if surprised by her attitude. ''You don't care if a guilty man goes free?''

''Lots of guilty men go free,'' she said, thinking of all the men she'd grown up around who she now realized had been guilty as sin.

''We'll make the trade,'' he said after he'd turned onto the highway. ''We'll get your daughter back, but if staying out of your way means letting the kidnapper go, we might have a problem.''

She eyed him in the flickering light of the street lamps flashing past. ''You should know, if I get the opportunity, I intend to take the ledger back and make the trade without your interference. I'll do whatever I have to do to get my daughter back. Including stopping you from risking her life just so you can play hero and bring in the bad guy in the name of justice.''

He shook his head at her. "You are something, you know that? I have *both* weapons, I have you and the ledger and you're telling me how it's going to be?"

"I won't let you jeopardize my daughter's life," she repeated.

"Being J. B. Crowe's only grandchild has already done that," he retorted.

She couldn't argue that, but soon she and her daughter would have new names, new identities, new lives. It wouldn't be easy to escape her father and his legacy. Amanda might still have his blood running through her veins, but she wouldn't be J. B. Crowe's daughter ever again. And Susannah would never know about her grandfather, the mobster.

The thought make her sad. But it was J.B.'s own fault that he was about to lose his daughter—and granddaughter.

But first she had to get Susannah back and that was becoming more difficult all the time, she thought looking over at Jesse. Especially since he didn't believe that Kincaid had kidnapped her baby.

AS HE DROVE through the thick Texas night toward Red River, he felt as if he'd been heading in this direction all his life. His life must have begun there. And it was there he would find out the truth.

But what was the truth? And was it something he could live with?

He couldn't help but feel disloyal to his family, the people who had loved him and raised him. And torn. He was a cop. Going to Red River, digging into the past, finding out the truth. It all made sense to the cop in him.

But still he felt guilty. He should be thankful for everything Pete and Marie McCall had done for him.

Unfortunately, he couldn't forget the copy of the newspaper clipping. Nor could he not worry about the person who'd put it under his door at the Crowe compound. He had to go to Red River. He had to uncover the truth. It was the kind of man he was. Come hell or high water.

He used Amanda's cell phone to call his boss at home, waking him up, to tell him that he was headed for Red River. His boss hadn't been happy to hear it since Jesse didn't offer any explanation. But he felt someone should know where he was.

To make matters worse, he had to worry about keeping himself and Amanda alive.

He had the ledger and Amanda Crowe. Having either could get him killed. Having both was suicide.

If that wasn't bad enough, Amanda would be looking for an opening to take the ledger back the first chance she got. He'd have to sleep with one eye open. Or not sleep at all until they made the trade.

He glanced over at her. She had settled into her seat as if nothing could budge her from his side. He was sure that was true as long as he had the ledger.

Nor did he plan on letting her out of his sight. That meant they'd be inseparable. And he knew how dangerous that would be.

"You don't believe me, do you?" she said.

He didn't really want to get into this with her but he could hear the determination in her voice and by now he knew when she wasn't going to let something go.

"I understand why you believe that Kincaid is behind this," he said. The kidnapper wanted a ledger that would damage Crowe—maybe even destroy him. Of course, Amanda would suspect Governor Thomas Kincaid. After all, Kincaid's campaign platform had been to eradicate the mob—more accurately, his nemesis, J. B. Crowe.

But kidnapping? It seemed awfully risky for a man in Kincaid's position. And the bottom line was, if Kincaid got caught, it would do more than just destroy his career. He wouldn't last long in prison, not after all the men he'd sent up as a former district attorney. Kincaid was a man known for being tough on criminals.

"You know Kincaid is the kidnapper for a fact?" he asked, all cop again.

"You mean can I prove it?" she asked bristling at his tone. "Not yet. But based on everything I know about the kidnapper, yes. It's Kincaid. Who else would ask for the ledger as ransom?"

"Any enemy your father ever made who now wants to bring him down," Jesse suggested. "And I would imagine J.B.'s made quite a few."

"You don't understand. My father and Governor Kincaid are at war. Diana and I and our babies are just casualties of that war."

He could hear the anger in her voice, the tears just behind them. "It isn't unusual for a governor to want to get rid of the mob," he said quietly.

She gave him a pitying look. "You really think that's what this is about? My father and Kincaid have a history that goes back to when they were boys growing up in Dallas—on the wrong side of the tracks, so to speak."

Hadn't he suspected as much? "What kind of history?"

She sighed. "Kincaid had a little brother, Billy. Billy and my father were best friends, inseparable as kids and later teenagers. Unfortunately, Thomas Kincaid wasn't happy about their relationship. He knew my father did errands for members of the Organization. He didn't want his little brother getting involved with the mob."

She took a breath and met his gaze. "My father swears that Billy wasn't involved in anything illegal, in fact, Billy was trying to get J.B. to go to college. Billy thought my father would have made a great lawyer." She smiled at this.

"What happened?" Jesse said, knowing it could only have ended badly.

"Billy was killed. Shot down by cops during a convenience store robbery that went bad." She shook her head, anticipating his next question. "My father had nothing to do with the robbery. Nor anyone in the Organization. He was devastated. He loved Billy. And he blamed the cops and Kincaid. You see, Kincaid saw the neighborhood market being robbed that night and called the police not knowing J.B. and Billy were inside. Afterward, Kincaid blamed J.B. because of his friendship with Billy. Kincaid was convinced J.B. had something to do with the robbery. Kincaid became governor. My father became a mobster. The rest is history."

Jesse let out a low whistle. That definitely could explain some of the animosity between J.B. and Kincaid.

"Now do you understand why my father and Kincaid are obsessed with destroying each other at any cost?" she asked.

He still found it hard to believe that Kincaid would do anything to jeopardize his career—let alone his life—to get J. B. Crowe after all these years, but at least Jesse better understood now why Amanda believed it.

They drove in silence for a few miles.

"By the way, my name's not Brock," he told her. "It's McCall. Jesse McCall. At least it was when I went undercover two weeks ago."

Chapter Ten

They drove through what little remained of the night, stopping only for gas for the van or coffee to stay awake. Amanda wasn't the least bit sleepy. She watched the dark landscape blur past and thought of Susannah. Had it only been a little over three days since Susannah had been kidnapped? It seemed like weeks. She should have been holding her daughter in her arms right now, not traveling across the state of Texas with an undercover cop. She ached with the need.

She had cried so many tears, she felt as if the well had gone dry. Soon, she told herself. Soon, she would have her daughter. Only the next time, she wouldn't let anything go wrong because she would be alone and in control of the trade. She had no intention of putting Susannah's welfare in Jesse's hands. Even if he was a cop.

That meant getting the ledger and that would

mean getting rid of Jesse Brock—McCall, she corrected.

In the meantime, she had little choice but to go along with him. He had the ledger and her daughter's life in his hands. Temporarily.

She felt a moment of guilt. She'd seen how desperately he'd wanted to take the ledger to the cops. But he hadn't. And for that she was grateful. They still had a long way to go until she was contacted for another trade. Jesse might weaken. Or she might get the ledger away from him. A lot could happen.

She thought about what would happen after the trade. The new life she would make with Susannah. For Susannah. She clung to that.

"I think you should call your father." It was the first thing Jesse had said in miles.

"You have to be kidding," she said incredulous. "And tell him what?"

"He might think you've been kidnapped."

"You mean I haven't?" she asked sarcastically.

"I'm serious. Tell him you're all right. That you're being held in protective custody for twenty-four hours."

"You are serious," she said studying him.

"He's your father," Jesse said. "He'll be worried."

She nodded, wondering just how worried her father would be as she pulled out her cell phone. Her father answered in the first ring. "It's me."

"Amanda, my God, I have been out of my mind with worry," he said, sounding like he meant it.

"I'm sorry. It's a long story. All I can tell you is that I'm all right."

He was silent for a long moment.

She thought he might be crying. J. B. Crowe? She must be hallucinating from lack of sleep. "Don't look for me, all right? I'll call you in twenty-four hours. I'm...okay." She hung up, shaken.

"Well?" Jesse asked.

"He took it well," she said, wondering how many men he'd sent out trying to find her. Or if he'd do as she'd asked and call them off.

Jesse slowed the van at the Red River city limits sign and she wondered for the first time what they were doing here. It was the intensity of his expression as he drove into the dusty, little town that suddenly had her worried. What was this about?

He made a pass through town. It didn't take but a few minutes. Main Street was only a few blocks long. Bank, grocery, gas station, café, newspaper, dry goods store.

She was looking at the small sleeping town, wondering what it would be like to raise a daughter in a place like this when Jesse pulled up in front of the *Red River Weekly* and cut the engine.

He glanced over at her. "You can stay in the car if you want."

Yeah, right. "I go where the ledger goes," she said.

"That's going to make bathing interesting," he said as he climbed out of the van, locking it behind him.

The thought had its appeal. In fact, it was the first pleasing thought she'd had in hours. She smiled and followed after him.

He tried the door to the newspaper office, but it was too early according to the sign in the window. "How about some breakfast?"

As far as she was concerned, it was also way too early for breakfast, but she could use more coffee. She watched the reflection of the street in the windows of the businesses as they walked the half block down to the Lariat Café and realized she and Susannah would stand out too much in a town like this. She'd thought about nothing else but how to disappear once she had her daughter.

A bell chimed as Jesse pushed open the door. It was cool inside, the interior sparse. Only a few well-worn tables and chairs sat on the black-and-white-tiled linoleum between a short row of booths and the lunch counter.

Several older men hunched over coffee cups on the blue vinyl stools along the counter. They turned as she and Jesse entered and kept watching as he led her to a booth. She slid into the vinyl and felt a chill. Was there any chance her father had contacts this far north? It didn't seem likely. But of course the governor's extended across the entire state.

The men at the stools finally turned back to their conversation and their cups.

"Howdy," said a pert older waitress as she slid two glasses of ice water and two plastic-covered menus across the marred tabletop. "Get ya'll some coffee?"

"Please," Amanda said. She would have killed for a latte but she could see that strong and black, straight from the pot, was all she was going to get in this town.

The waitress plopped a cup and saucer down in front of her and poured. Amanda took a sip and grimaced.

"Not the expensive Colombian blend you're used to?" Jesse asked wryly after the waitress left.

"You really think I'm just a spoiled kid, don't you?"

He raised a brow in answer.

She would have loved to argue differently but it was true. "All that's going to change," she said taking another drink of the coffee and this time not making a face.

"How will you live once you leave?" he enquired.

She could detect only a faint touch of sarcasm in his tone as she met his gaze over the top of her cup. "I plan to *work*. I might not be able to use my degree but I can find something in my field."

"And what field would that be? Art history? Philosophy? Or maybe interpretive dance?"

"Electrical engineering."

His jaw dropped.

She smiled and took another sip of her coffee. It wasn't so bad, after all. "How do you think I was able to get the ledger with all the hidden cameras and the security system at the house?" He was staring at her as if he'd never seen her before. His look was different. Not sexual. More like just plain interested in her.

She felt a little buzz at the thought and smiled to herself. Maybe Jesse was starting to see her as a person, more than just female body parts. The thought brightened her day because it had obviously upset him—and the closer she got to him, the harder it would be for him to be a cop, and not a man.

And the easier it would be for her to get the ledger back and make the trade—without him.

Jesse discreetly took the ledger from his pocket and opened it, thumbing slowly through the pages. She watched him. His strong jaw was dark with stubble, his eyes black as obsidian.

She'd never noticed the small curved scar over

his left eyebrow before and wondered how he'd gotten it. She knew so little about him—and yet so much, she thought. She knew how desperately he wanted to catch the kidnapper, to send her father to prison, to see that justice was done. It made her sad for him. In this world, there was little justice. She feared his battle was futile and would only bring him pain and disappointment.

He grew very quiet as he closed the ledger.

She waited for him to say something. He seemed lost in thought and not good thoughts from the look of him.

"You aren't still thinking of taking it to the police?" she asked hesitantly. It wasn't an option and she'd fight heaven and hell to stop him from it.

She was relieved when he shook his head.

"No," he said. "I told you I would let you use it to get your daughter back. You'll find I stick to my promises."

She looked down at her menu, almost feeling guilty about her plans to keep him from the trade. Almost.

She studied her menu, antsy. Hers was a waiting game now. Waiting for Gage to set up the next trade. Waiting for Jesse to slip up and give her the opportunity to get the ledger back and get away.

She glanced up at him. If he wanted to play detective in the meantime, what did she care? He was looking at the ledger again, his brows furrowed in a frown. Everything about him looked dangerous. But as she studied him she sensed the only thing she had to fear was the desire he invoked within her.

When the waitress returned, Jesse ordered chicken fried steak, grits and biscuits with milk gravy. Amanda ordered a Spanish omelette. She'd never liked breakfast—especially at this hour.

"So what made you become a cop?" she asked as they ate. She hadn't realized how hungry she was and the omelette was good, the sauce hot and spicy and just what she needed.

"I don't know," he said after a moment. "I guess I believe in justice."

She should have known.

"You don't like authority figures, do you?" he asked between bites.

Did anyone? "I'll admit I had some bad experiences with cops as a child. It might have prejudiced my feelings."

"Maybe I can change that," he said.

Don't hold your breath, she thought, but when she looked up and met his gaze, she said, "Maybe. So tell me about yourself," she said as she studied him, wondering about him more than she wanted to.

He shrugged. "I was raised north of Dallas on a lake. I have," he seemed to hesitate, "two brothers and three sisters."

She lifted a brow. "That's a big family. I'm envious."

He nodded. "Yeah, they're really something. You'd like them." He flushed as if realizing too late that she would never have a reason to meet them.

"And your parents?" she asked, betting they were still together.

"My father is an accountant and my mother is a substitute grade school teacher," he said slowly.

She blinked. "Wow, can't get much more normal than that. Your mother probably volunteers at the hospital and bakes bread for the food bank."

He shook his head. "She volunteers at the senior center and makes quilts for the poor."

She laughed.

"My family is very dull by your standards," he said and turned his attention to his breakfast.

"I would love dull, believe me." She didn't want to get on the subject of her so-called family. "So, let me guess, you were very popular in high school, star quarterback of the football team and..." She squinted at him. "King of the senior prom and your date, the queen of the prom, was named...Brittany."

He looked up from his breakfast, humor in his eyes as he smiled at her. He had a great smile. "You're wrong. Her name was Tiffany."

Amanda laughed. "I knew it."

"What about you?" he asked, his gaze turning serious.

"I was one of the nerds, the .com, chess club, honor roll crowd."

"No prom?"

"Not my thing," she said, surprised how defensive she sounded. "I was your classic Stephen King Carrie."

"I really doubt that. I'm sure there were lots of guys who wanted to ask you but were intimidated. And I don't blame them," Jesse said.

"Because of my father," she said, dismissing his comment.

"No, because you were the smartest, prettiest girl in the school."

She eyed him suspiciously, but couldn't help but smile. "Okay, what do you want?" she asked, only half joking.

"You already know what I want," he said, his heated gaze warming her to her toes. "I told you during one of my weaker, more honest moments."

"More than you want to put my father in jail?"

"More than even that," he said.

She laughed, but her gaze never left his face. Like him, she was only too aware of the chemistry between them. Worse, the more she was around him, the more she was starting to like him.

After breakfast while Jesse paid the check, she stepped outside for some fresh air. The street was still practically empty, the town slumbering in the warming sun.

She waited, feeling anxious. She just wanted her daughter. The ache in her heart felt heavy as stone. She tried not to think of Susannah's smile. Or her bright eyes. Or the way she curled her tiny fingers around Amanda's finger. Her baby.

Jesse came out of the café and looked around for her as if he thought she might have taken off. Not likely.

As they walked down the street to the *Red River Weekly,* he seemed as nervous and anxious as she felt. And wary. He appeared to be studying the faces of the people they passed as if looking for something. She realized how exposed they were in a town like this. Easy pickings.

A young woman looked up from her desk as they walked into the newspaper office.

"Can I help you?" she asked, peering at them through a pair of pink-framed glasses. Her eyes were lined in black, her cheeks two startling red slashes of blush. A necklace of blue plastic beads noosed her neck above a T-shirt and jeans. Around her floated an aura of grape-flavored bubble gum and open curiosity. The name plate on her desk read: Aimee Carruthers.

"I'd like to take a look at your morgue," Jesse said.

"What year are ya'll interested in?" she asked, studying them intently through her glasses.

"June, 1971."

Aimee Carruthers looked surprised.

Not as surprised as Amanda.

The woman recovered quickly and got to her feet. "June, 1971?" She seemed to wait for Jesse to say more, but he didn't and finally she led them back to a small room.

The morgue had only one window, which was thankfully hanging open. A faint breeze hardly rustled the papers on the top of a filing cabinet under it, but made the tiny warm room bearable.

"That'd be on microfiche." Aimee motioned to a set of small metal drawers each labeled with dates. "You know how to work it?" she asked.

Jesse nodded. "Thanks."

It was obvious she didn't want to leave the room, but it was equally obvious Jesse wasn't going to start his search until she did.

"If ya'll need any help—"

"We'll holler," he said, cutting her off.

She left but not before propping the door open to give them a little more air. Right.

The moment the nosy Aimee Carruthers was gone, he pulled out the drawer labeled 1971 and extracted the spool of film that contained June.

Amanda walked over to the window and looked out onto the alley. The air smelled of red Texas dust and sunshine. When she turned, Jesse was staring at the screen. A headline caught her eye: Infant Abandoned Beside Road.

JESSE'S HEART jerked at the sight of the familiar headline. He scanned the story he now knew by heart, then moved on to the next week. Amanda had moved closer and now stood at his side watching the screen. Behind him he heard a sound, a popping of gum and the scent of grape.

He didn't need to turn around. He knew Aimee Carruthers had probably seen the article on the screen. He also realized it would be impossible to keep anything a secret in a town this size—especially once he started asking questions. He would just have to find the answers fast.

In the next week's paper he found only a brief piece on page one about the baby: Parents of Abandoned Infant Sought. It was followed by a plea by Sheriff Art Turner for the mother to come forward.

The article said the baby had been found in a cardboard box, wrapped in a pale blue blanket on Woodland Lake Road. Like the first story, the article didn't mention the gold chain or the strange heart-shaped pendant found on the baby or the name of the person who'd discovered the newborn beside the road.

Amanda pulled up a chair and sat down beside him as she read the article. Out of the corner of his eye, he saw her frown at the screen, then at him, but she said nothing as he scrolled the pages of the next week's paper.

The story of the infant had dropped to the third page. There was only a short piece titled, No Leads On Found Baby. The investigation had stalled. No one had come forward.

He moved to the next weekly paper but found no mention of the infant. Nor was there anything in the next paper. Or the next. He scanned the rest of June, July, August, all the way to December, 1971. The baby boy left beside the road had been forgotten.

So how had his parents come to adopt him?

Slowly, he turned back to the last story and re-read it, finding nothing new of interest except that the baby had been found a quarter mile down the road from the old Duncan place.

He made copies of the stories with a growing uneasiness as he recalled his parents' reluctance to even talk about the night they'd found him beside that road. And their repeated concerns that he not dig in the past.

Aimee Carruthers was on the phone when they came out of the newspaper morgue. She stopped talking and gave them a nervous smile as she held her hand over the mouthpiece until they were out the door. When Jesse looked back she was hunched over the phone, talking hurriedly. He wondered how long it would take for everyone in town to know.

He cut across the street with Amanda keeping stride beside him. She didn't ask and he was grateful, but as he opened the door of city hall for her, he saw her look of concern and remembered her dislike for cops and her fear that he'd turn the ledger over to the police.

"Trust me," he whispered.

Her look was half plea, half warning.

He'd hate to ever cross this woman.

The police station was an anteroom off city hall, just large enough for two desks. A skinny red-headed young man stood behind the short counter, his freckles seeming to leap off his pallid face. A pair of red-rimmed pale-blue eyes peered at them with obvious interest as they entered. He wore a deputy's uniform and his name tag read: Deputy Lane Waller.

Lane Waller had just hung up the phone. Jesse suspected that Aimee Carruthers had called him. Now why would she do that, he wondered with a growing uneasiness.

"I'm looking for Sheriff Art Tucker?" Jesse said stepping up to the counter, hoping that the sheriff might still be around after all these years.

"Well, he shouldn't be hard to find." On closer inspection, the young man didn't look old enough to drive, let alone carry the loaded weapon at his hip. "You can find him where he always is this time of day."

"And where might that be?" Jesse asked when the deputy didn't go on.

"Oak Rest Cemetery on the edge of town," Lane said and chuckled heartily at his own joke.

Funny. Jesse tried to squash his disappointment in the sheriff's demise, but after all it *had* been thirty years. "How about the coroner?" Jesse recalled his name from the newspaper article. "Gene Wells?"

Again Lane shook his head. "Pushing up daisies as well."

"I suppose there isn't anyone around still who worked in this office thirty years ago?" Jesse asked, feeling like he'd hit a dead end already.

Lane Waller chuckled. "Not unless you count Hubert Owens."

"Who is he?" Jesse asked.

"Tucker's former deputy but he's—"

"If he's still alive, where can I find him?" Jesse asked, before he could be assaulted by another of Lane Waller's bad jokes.

He glanced at his watch. "He should be having his third beer by now over at the Corral Bar. He might even be half sober. Or awake."

The Corral was wedged between the local garage and the drugstore. Rough-hewn cedar covered the front in a western-looking log fence design.

Beer signs glowed in the dusty window, illuminating a handful of spiky cactus plants covered with cobwebs and red Texas dust.

The bar was empty except for an elderly man on a stool, hunched over a glass of draft and a younger man washing glasses behind the bar. At the back, an old Patsy Cline tune played on the jukebox.

"Hubert Owens?" Jesse asked as he took the stool next to the man and Amanda pulled up one on the other side. Of course Amanda drew the man's attention.

Owens gave her a blurry, near toothless smile. "Most people just call me Huey," he said brightly and sat up a little straighter. He hadn't shaved in days and reeked of stale beer, sweat and tobacco.

"Mr. Owens, I understand you were a deputy in town thirty years ago," Jesse said.

Owens reluctantly turned to squint at Jesse, his look instantly suspicious. "What of it?"

"We're trying to find out about that little baby that was left near the old Duncan place thirty years ago," Amanda said turning on the charm, which was considerable. "Out on Woodland Lake Road?"

Hubert Owens swiveled his head back around to her. "Sure, sweetie, but what would a young thing like you care about that for?"

"I think that little baby might be someone I

know,'' she said, her brown eyes turning to gaze at Jesse challengingly. "You probably don't remember much about the case...."

"The heck I don't, little lady. 'Member it like it was yesterday. Strangest damn—'scuse me— strangest darned thing to happen around here."

Jesse sat back on his stool and watched Amanda in the mirror with a mixture of irritation, amusement and gratitude. She was smart enough to have put two and two together and figure out what he was looking for. His admiration of her grew.

"What was so strange about it?" she asked conspiratorially.

Owens leaned toward her. Jesse could smell his beer-soaked breath from where he sat and knew Amanda was getting the full force of it. Well, she'd asked for it.

"Who'd leave a little baby like that in a box beside the road?" the old man asked. "Didn't make no sense at all." He leaned closer to her. "And the note—" He shook his head.

"What note?" Jesse mouthed to Amanda in the mirror.

"There was a note?" she asked in a hushed, sexy voice.

The old man nodded smugly. "That part never got into the paper. Ya know ya always got to keep one piece of evidence back. That way when someone comes forward, wanting the baby, ya got something secret. If they can tell ya what's in the note, then—"

"What *was* in the note?" she asked trying to steer him back on track.

He glanced down the bar at the bartender. He didn't seem to be paying any attention but Jesse knew he was listening to every word.

"Guess after all these years it don't make no difference," Owens said. "And you seem like a nice enough girl." The old man seemed to zone out for a moment.

"Was the note handwritten?" Amanda prompted.

He blinked, then nodded. "Handwritten and kinda scrawled like the person writing it had been in a hurry. Said—and I'll never forget this—'Take care of my precious baby. I will go to my grave loving him.'"

The words squeezed at Jesse's heart.

"You probably had your suspicions about whose baby it was," Amanda said. "I mean, it would be hard in a town this size to hide being pregnant."

Jesse watched her work in the mirror, admiring how easily deception came to her. Must be something in the genes. The thought brought him up short as he wondered about his own genes.

Owens stared down into his beer. "Weren't no local gal, I can tell you that." Owens glanced over at Amanda. "You know, you're the second person who's asked about that baby. Couple weeks ago—" He seemed to catch himself. He reached for his beer and drained it.

"Who else was asking about the baby?" Jesse asked.

Owens didn't answer. He looked around the empty bar. The bartender was busy washing glasses and didn't look up.

Amanda laid a hand on the old man's arm. "Who else was asking?" she whispered.

"That's just it," Owens said, dropping his voice. "What's a guy like that coming around here asking a lot of questions after all these years about some baby? Makes people nervous, you know. Ain't like we all ain't seen him in the paper."

"A guy like what?" Amanda asked.

Owens fidgeted on his stool for a moment, then looked over at her. Jesse watched in the mirror behind the bar as the old man whispered one word, "Mobster."

Jesse's eyes met Amanda's in the mirror. He'd seen her tense at the word, some of the color draining from her face.

"Which mobster?" she asked in a small strained voice.

"That Crowe fella, but you didn't hear that from me," Owens said and pounded on the bar with his empty glass. "If that couple was willing to take the baby, I don't see no reason to tell anyone about 'em. 'Specially someone like him.''

"You're sure it was J. B. Crowe?'' Amanda persisted.

"The one that's in the paper today,'' Owens said, sounding scared. "You think I don't know who I talked to? You think I don't know about that underworld stuff?''

"What did you tell him?'' Amanda asked, a tremor in her voice.

"Don't know nothin','' the old man muttered, swaying a little on the stool. "Nothin' 'bout that couple that found the baby. Nothin' 'bout no baby. Nothin' at all.'' He winked at her, then his head dropped to the bar and he began to snore loudly.

The bartender came down to take Owens's glass. He didn't say a word but Jesse noticed how he also didn't meet his eyes as if he didn't want to get involved.

Behind them the door banged open. A man in a sheriff's uniform filled the door frame. He was large, his expression displeased. "I heard there might be a problem over here?'' he said eyeing them.

The bartender shook his head. "No problem here, Sheriff Wilson.''

Sheriff Wilson let his gaze run over Jesse, then slowed as it took in Amanda. The only sound in the room was Hubert "Huey'' Owens's loud snoring.

Jesse got to his feet, figuring now was as good as any time to talk to the sheriff. But the man's wide face closed over. He tipped his hat to Amanda, then turned around and left as if in a hurry.

"What was that about?" she asked after the door had banged shut behind the sheriff.

"Beats me." Nor did Jesse plan to take it up with the sheriff. At least not now. He followed Amanda out of the bar. "Thanks for your help in there. You were good," he admitted grudgingly.

"No problem," she said and walked over to the curb. "Wanna tell me about it?"

"Not really," he said. "Not yet."

She nodded.

"Also I wouldn't take too much of what the guy said to heart," he told her, knowing all that mobster talk had upset her. "The baby was only a few hours old. Of course it was a local girl's. And that stuff about him recognizing the mobster from the paper—"

"Jesse."

Something in her tone stopped him. He joined her at the curb and saw that she was staring down at one of the newspaper racks. The *Dallas Morning News*.

Looking out from the front page was J. B. Crowe. He'd just been given some humanitarian award in Dallas.

Chapter Eleven

An icy chill ran up his spine. Could J. B. Crowe have been in Red River? Asking about the baby? Asking about Jesse? But why?

He grabbed Amanda's arm and ushered her quickly across the street to the van. It wasn't until they were both inside that he said, "Right after I went to work for your father, he made a business trip." He heard the fear in his voice. "Do you know where he went?"

She shook her head. "I just know he was upset when he got back. What's going on?"

Jesse started the van. "I wish I knew."

At the town's only gas station, he called Dylan from the pay phone outside. He'd forgotten that Dylan said he would be on another case and out for a while. Dylan's sister Lily gave him the news, though. The fingerprints had come back on the photocopy of the newspaper article Jesse had given

Dylan. There was a second set of prints on the paper. J. B. Crowe's.

Jesse stood for a moment in the phone booth, his heart pounding. J. B. Crowe had been up here two weeks ago asking about a baby left by the road thirty years before. Then he put the photocopy of the newspaper article under Jesse's door. Why?

Inside the classic old filling station, Jesse asked directions to Woodland Lake Road and the old Duncan place. The attendant eyed them warily as he pointed east, seemingly glad when the van pulled away from his pumps.

They quickly left the small town behind, the road running red to the horizon. Not far out, they picked up a creek. It twisted and turned its way through the brush beside the road, the day already growing hot and no shade except for a small puddle beneath the occasional tree they passed. Behind the van, dust boiled up into the faded blue of the Texas sky, the landscape as bleak as his reason for driving out here.

He tried to steel himself at the thought of seeing the spot where he'd been abandoned. A building appeared ahead. The old farmhouse sat on the hill, weathered and gray, a faint sign on the fence, Duncan. The old Duncan place.

He drove past it, wanting to see the curve in the road beside the creek a quarter mile farther where, according to the newspaper article, the baby had been found.

A golden Texas sun beat down on the red earth and van as he coasted down the hill. Crickets chirped from the bushes beside the creek and in the distance a hawk cried as it circled overhead.

He could see the bend in the road ahead, the wide spot next to it and the creek.

He slowed the van, trying to imagine what had happened in the hours, the days, the years before he was left in this lonely, desolate spot.

Braking, he brought the van to a stop, killed the engine and slowly opened his door. He could feel Amanda's gaze on him. She had said little since they'd left the bar. As he walked toward where he imagined he'd been left that night, he heard her open her door and get out.

There was a low spot beside the creek and road the width of a car. He stepped into the shade of the largest of the trees, his heart hammering in his ears. This had to be the place. He could see it, the darkness, the car coming up the road, stopping and the door opening as someone lowered the cardboard box to the earth. The door of the car closing quickly. The sound of the engine dying away in the distance.

It sickened him, frightened him and made him angry and grief-stricken all at the same time. Why? Why would his mother have done such a thing? If she hadn't wanted him, why not leave him on someone's doorstep?

Because she hadn't wanted anyone to know she'd given birth to him. She hadn't expected him to survive. She hadn't expected someone to find him. Then why the note? And the gold chain with the odd-shaped heart?

He closed his eyes, breathing in the unfamiliar scents, listening to the sounds of water and rustling leaves and birds high in the branches. Anger and pain and a horrible sense of betrayal filled his heart to bursting. And fear. There was more to the story. He could feel it. A woman who didn't want her child didn't write a hurried note, didn't put a gold heart in the baby's blanket.

And now J. B. Crowe had been asking about the baby. Knew Jesse was the baby. Why else had J.B. given him the copy of the newspaper article?

"This baby we're looking for," Amanda said, dragging him from his thoughts. "It's you, isn't it?"

He opened his eyes. She was standing in front of him.

He blinked, fighting emotions that threatened to drop him to his knees. And he'd had the nerve to berate her for *her* genes. "Yeah." He told her about the McCalls, and how they had found him and raised him, about the copy of the newspaper clipping and the news that he was adopted.

"I'm sorry. You didn't know until yesterday?"
He shook his head.

"Oh, that must have been a terrible shock."

"You could say that." He was still reeling from it. And now to find out that J. B. Crowe put the copy of the newspaper article under his door. Worse, that J.B. had been in Red River asking questions about the baby.

"I don't know what to say." She reached over to squeeze his hand.

He didn't want her pity, but almost at once he realized that wasn't what she was offering.

"You and I have more in common than I would have ever thought," she said, looking at him as though seeing him differently now. "Only, I'd love to find out I was adopted."

She seemed to hesitate. "What does it have to do with my father?"

"I don't know." He met her gaze. "But I intend to find out."

He turned back to the van. That's when he saw the old Duncan place perched on the hill, caught the flash of the sun off one of the windows. He stopped and stared up at the house. "They could have seen it," he said. "Whoever lived there."

She followed his gaze and hugged herself as if suddenly cold. "It was at night, right? They could have seen the lights from the car. Maybe even seen the interior light come on."

He looked over at her, glad she was there with him. "I think I know who might have been living up there thirty years ago."

THE HOUSE had seen better days and the yard was filled with falling-down outbuildings and broken-down equipment and vehicles.

Jesse slowed the van, his heart a hammer in his chest. His parents had warned him not to dig in the past. Obviously something had frightened them.

He pulled off onto the dirt track, the bumper of the van slapping down the tall weeds, and drove up to the house. Turning off the engine, he sat for a moment, listening. Crickets chirped in the tall grass, a hawk screeched overhead and, closer, he could hear a bee droning just outside the window.

The house was empty and looked as if it had been for some time. He opened his door. He didn't know why, but he needed to go inside the old rambling farmhouse. He needed to know how Marie and Pete McCall had found him. He had a pretty good idea that he was right about one thing at least.

"You might want to wait here." He'd half expected Amanda to argue.

"All right," she agreed, her gaze on the creepy old place.

Like him, she seemed to feel wary of the place. Just something in the air. A disquiet. A feeling of foreboding. As if some presence remained, a memory of something awful that had happened.

Jesse tried to shake off the feeling as he stared at the blank darkness where windows should have been on the second floor. Most of the glass was gone, leaving yawning openings and the dusty woven webs of spiders in the window frames.

He pushed open the already ajar door and was hit with the cold putrid breath of the house. He hesitated, telling himself there was nothing to be learned here. Dust and debris coated the worn wooden floor. A scurrying sound came from a distant room.

He peered into what had once been the dining room, the floor creaking under his weight. There were old clothes and books and newspapers and magazines piled in a corner. He dug a newspaper out of one pile and looked at the date. Newer than 1971.

He thought he heard a car engine. But knew it wasn't the van. He'd taken the key. And even if Amanda had another set, she wouldn't leave without the ledger in his pocket.

He moved deeper into the house where the shadows hunkered, dark and cold in corners. Something moved off to his right, making him jump. A rat scampered from a pile of clothing, disappearing around the corner into the next room.

As he climbed the rickety stairs to the second

floor, he asked himself what he was looking for. Hadn't he seen enough of this place? He stopped in one of the old bedrooms. A rusted metal box spring mattress leaned against one wall, a pair of once blue curtains fluttered at the broken window, on the floor was a book with a watermarked brown cover.

He bent down to pick it up. An old Hardy Boy's mystery, one he'd read as a boy, *The Secret of the Old Mill.* The pages smelled of mildew and dust as he flipped it open, trying to remember the story, trying to think of anything but the reason he was here.

Inside the cover of the book was stamped Red River Community Library. He flipped to the back and pulled out the library card. The book was long overdue. Thirty years worth. But he could still read the name of the person who'd checked it out. Marie McCall. His adoptive mother.

The wooden steps of the stairs creaked. He froze, listening. Another step creaked and another. Goose bumps skittering over his skin like a spider's legs. Someone was coming up the stairs.

"Amanda?"

No answer.

"Amanda?" he called a little louder as he moved back toward the stairs. Suddenly he wished he hadn't left her alone in the van. Not after everything they'd learned here.

He dropped the book and drew the weapon he'd taken from Amanda yesterday. Slowly, he crept down the hall toward the stairs. As he came to the corner, he heard the stairs at the top creak and saw a shadow spill across the landing floor. Not Amanda. Too tall and broad for her.

"Hello?" came a male voice, one he recognized just in time.

Hurriedly, he shoved the gun back into the waistband of his jeans and covered it with his shirt just as Sheriff Wilson topped the stairs.

"Ya know ya'll are trespassing?" the sheriff asked with obvious irritation.

"Just having a look around," Jesse said.

The sheriff nodded. "I heard you've been just looking around and asking a lot of questions, upsetting a lot of people."

Jesse wanted to take this conversation outside into the sunlight, away from this house and everything in it, especially that presence that he'd felt, a presence like an albatross around his neck.

He did wonder, though, just who he'd been upsetting and why.

"Who are you and what business brings you to Red River?" Wilson demanded.

Jesse thought about telling the sheriff that he was a cop out of Dallas up here investigating the mob. But how would he explain Amanda? The last thing he wanted was the sheriff to know who she was. If the cop didn't already.

"Sheriff, I just learned that I might have been that mystery baby that was found around here thirty years ago." Jesse suspected he wasn't telling the sheriff anything he didn't already know. "I just want to find out who I am."

"No one around here knows. Or cares," the sheriff said with a coldness that surprised Jesse.

"My mother had to be one of the local girls—"

The sheriff was shaking his head. "Whoever left that baby wasn't from around here."

"How do you know that?" Jesse asked.

"You'll just have to take my word for it." The sheriff moved toward him, his hand on the butt of his weapon, a steely hardness in his eyes that made Jesse want to retreat a step.

"Jesse?" Amanda called from the floor below.

"Honey, I'm up here. I'll be right down," Jesse called out quickly. "My fiancée and I are on our way to get married in Oklahoma," he improvised and hoped Amanda went for it. "Her mama lives up there," he said loud enough he thought Amanda would hear.

He moved to get past the sheriff, but Wilson was a big man, thick through the chest with a head like a block of wood. The cop didn't budge and for a moment Jesse feared he wasn't going to.

"Jesse?" Amanda called again, definite concern in her voice.

"Up here, honey," he called again. "Stay there, I'm coming down. Those stairs are dangerous." He looked at the sheriff. "I thought it was important that I find out about myself before I got married," he said.

"Let me give you a little advice," the sheriff said quietly. "Some things are best left alone."

Jesse nodded. "I'm beginning to think you might be right about that."

"You can take it to the bank," the sheriff said and seemed relieved Jesse was seeing it his way. He stepped aside and let Jesse descend the steps to where Amanda waited, looking scared. She'd changed into other clothing from the back of the van. She now wore a silk shirt, slacks, sandals.

Jesse reached for her, realizing the sheriff was right behind him and could hear anything he said.

"Sorry, honey, I just got to looking around and lost track of time." He pulled Amanda into his arms. She came easily as if he'd held her like this a hundred times. "I guess we'd better get going if we hope to make your mama's before dark." He let go of her and stepped back, meeting her gaze.

"Where'd you say you were going in Oklahoma?" Sheriff Wilson asked Amanda.

"Lawton," she answered without hesitation, before shifting her gaze back to Jesse. "And we're going to be late, thanks to you. You know Mama's making dinner for us.''

He put his arm around her shoulders and pulled her close, grateful she was such a quick study. ''The last thing I want is to make your mama mad at me,'' he said with a laugh. Then he sobered as he glanced around the farmhouse. ''Nothing here, anyway.'' Nothing but ghosts.

The sheriff settled his ham-size fists on his hips. ''Glad to hear you're not planning to stay around,'' he said pointedly. ''I assume you won't be coming back to Red River?''

Jesse shook his head. ''We thought we'd honeymoon up north somewhere. Maybe Montana.''

Sheriff Wilson nodded, his look colder than the inside of the old house as he walked past Jesse, headed for the door. ''A good place for your kind.''

Jesse felt a chill soul deep. His kind. ''And what kind would that be, Sheriff?'' he asked the cop's broad back.

But Sheriff Wilson either didn't hear, or didn't care to answer.

''Bastard,'' Amanda swore under her breath at the sheriff's retreating back.

Jesse walked her to the van without a word, opened the door for her, then climbed into the driver's seat. Sheriff Wilson stood by his car, watching them, waiting for them to leave.

"What the hell was that about?" Jesse demanded, looking over at Amanda. She had angry tears in her eyes.

"He thinks you're the son of a mobster," she said. She looked over at him. "Don't you see? My father was here asking about the baby. The sheriff thinks you're J. B. Crowe's son."

Chapter Twelve

Jesse swore as he turned the van around and headed down the rutted path to the two-lane county road.

"I can see it in your face," Amanda said, her emotions raw and too close to the surface. Her chest ached from trying to hold back the well of feeling inside her. She wanted to strike out. Not at the sheriff. She'd met enough people like him in her life that she didn't care what he thought of her and her "kind." But Jesse—

"You're scared to death you might be the spawn of a mobster," she said, daring him to disagree.

He glanced over at her as he turned toward Red River and accelerated. The Texas sun-baked red dust kicked up behind the van, dark as a thunderhead.

Jesse's knuckles were white on the steering wheel, his jaw set in granite. She saw him glance in his rearview mirror, but she didn't need to turn to feel the sheriff's scornful gaze. She'd seen enough of them in her life.

"Frightening, isn't it," she said, her voice breaking. "After all the contempt you've had for me since the day you went to work for my father, just to think that you might have the same tainted blood as me."

He hit the brakes. The van went into a skid, coming to a stop in a cloud of red dust.

Before she could take a breath, he grabbed her and jerked her around to face him, his eyes dark with emotion. "You think I don't want to be related to you because of your genes?" he demanded loudly.

"Isn't that your greatest fear?" she cried, grabbing a handful of his shirt.

He let out a low growl, anger making his eyes as black as obsidian and just as bright. "Oh, yeah, that's a fear all right. I sure as hell don't want to be related to you. But not for the reasons you think."

She could see the pain in his eyes, his desire for her, his fear that she might always be forbidden to him. What surprised her was her own fear. She clung to his shirt, desperately wanting to tell him that he wasn't the only one hurting by this news.

He pushed her away from him before she could release her hold on his shirt. She heard the fabric tear and him let out a curse. Something fell out of his shirt pocket, making a slight tinkling sound as it dropped to the floor.

She watched him pick up the gold chain. It glistened for a moment in the sunlight. Long enough for her to see what dangled from the chain. She gasped at the sight of the unique-shaped heart, one she'd seen before.

He looked over at her. "What?" he demanded, sounding scared. "You recognize it?"

"My father has the other piece of the heart."

He stared at her, all his fears exploding like a bomb inside his head. "Your father has the *other* piece?"

She nodded. "He had the hearts made. There are only two like them in the world. They were made to fit together to form one heart. One perfect heart."

He barely heard her words, only the meaning behind them. His mother had put the gold heart in his blanket the night he was born and written a hurried note, hoping someone would find him. His father must have been the one who had left him in the box beside the road. The same man who had the matching gold heart.

"Then your father—"

She shook her head. "The heart belonged to my father's best friend." She seemed to pause as if for effect. "My father had the heart made for Billy Kincaid and the woman he was in love with."

"Billy Kincaid," he echoed.

"The Governor's little brother."

"The one who died," Jesse said.

She nodded. "When I was a little girl, I found a box with some old things in it. I was taken with the funny-shaped heart and my father told me the story."

They both turned at the sound of the vehicle coming up the road behind them. In the distance, the sun shimmered off the sheriff's car.

"Drive," she ordered. "We don't want another run-in with him."

Jesse couldn't have agreed more but he also desperately needed to know about the heart. He pulled back onto the road, his hands shaking. He wasn't J.B.'s son. He wasn't related to Amanda. Was she as relieved as he was? He glanced over at her.

She smiled and nodded. "I assume we are both relieved for the same reason."

"Both?"

She grinned. "Both."

"I also assume you want to hear about the heart first?" she asked.

"First?"

She laughed. "First." She glanced behind them. He followed her gaze. The sheriff's car had disappeared in their dust. "My father knew a jeweler and had the hearts made as a present for Billy and his girlfriend. He didn't want any others ever made like them so my father talked the jeweler into promising he never would. It was a promise I am sure the jeweler kept,'' she said knowingly.

Jesse had to agree.

''Billy and his girlfriend each wore one. The idea was that they would put the hearts together when they got married and he would put the one heart on her during the ceremony.''

''But then Billy got killed.''

She nodded. ''Obviously before they could get married.''

He drove through Red River almost without noticing and took the two-lane south, not sure where he was going, just far from the small Texas town.

''Who was the girlfriend?'' he asked, holding his breath.

''My father never told me. I got the feeling that Billy had kept the romance quiet for some reason. I'm not even sure my father knew her well.''

Was it possible J.B. hadn't known the girl was pregnant with Billy's son? He felt the skin on his neck prickle. The day J.B. had hired him— Jesse hadn't thought anything about it at the time. But J.B. had seemed in shock. Of course he would have been shocked; he'd believed his daughter had almost been killed by a hit-and-run driver.

But Jesse remembered now the way J.B. had stared at him. Almost as if the man had seen a ghost.

Ahead Jesse could see the outline of the town on the horizon. He'd be glad when it was in his rearview mirror.

"I know this sounds nuts, but I think your father recognized me that first day I went to work for him," Jesse said. "I think that's why he hired me, no questions asked. Why he left on a business trip the next day. He came to Red River. Started asking questions about me."

"That would explain the warm reception we've gotten here. I'm sure having a well-known mobster show up in town ruffled a few feathers, especially all the times my father's picture has been in the paper for one criminal investigation or another," she said.

He nodded. It would also explain J.B.'s fingerprints on the photocopy of the newspaper clipping. "Maybe he *didn't* know I existed until a couple of weeks ago. Or maybe he's the one who dumped the box beside the road for Billy, just assuming I would die."

"No," Amanda said with more force than he'd expected. "My father loved Billy like a brother. If he'd known about you, there isn't any way he would have allowed anything to happen to you, believe me. I know my father. He would have raised you himself."

He did believe her. "We have to find my mother," he said and looked over at her.

She nodded. "Jesse, I did lie about one thing."

The expression on her face almost made him drive off the road.

"I lied when I said I felt nothing but contempt for you." Leaning toward him, she put her hand on his thigh.

This time he did drive off the road. "Amanda?" He got the van under control again. "I'm a cop," he reminded her.

"And probably a Kincaid," she said. "And I'm a mobster's daughter. Nothing's really changed, has it?"

He shook his head. She was still dangerous and he still wanted her, wanted her more than he could have believed possible. "Nothing at all," he said and took the next side road down into the lush thick trees beside the river.

HER FINGERS trembled as she began to unbutton his shirt the moment he stopped the van beside the river.

"Amanda?"

"I need you, Jesse. I need you to hold me. To make love to me."

She touched a finger to his lips and shook her head. She knew all the reasons they shouldn't make love and one very good reason they should. As she slipped each button free, she exposed more of his muscular chest, his broad shoulders. Dark hair formed a V like an arrow to the waistband of his jeans. Desire stole through her, leaving a trail of heat to her center.

She wanted this man. Wanted his arms around her. Wanted to feel his bare skin pressed to hers. Wanted him in a primitive, carnal way, to possess and be possessed. And had for a long time.

That in itself scared her. She had never let any man close to her. Certainly not Gage, even though he'd fathered her baby.

With Jesse, it would be total surrender.

He looked at her as if afraid to touch her for fear of what they would do together, both wanting the same thing, both fearing it.

She leaned over and kissed him, her lips barely brushing his. ''I think there's a blanket in the back,'' she whispered.

The river lapped at the shore under a canopy of green leaves. He spread the blanket on the grass. Water pooled next to the bank. He looked at her, the desire in his gaze almost as pleasurable as the anticipation of his touch.

He reached out to undo the top button on her shirt, his fingers grazing her skin. His eyes never left hers as he undid the next button, then the next.

Her heart pounded as he slipped the shirt from her shoulders and let it drop to the blanket, then slipped off one strap of her bra, then the other. Her nipples pressed hard and insistent against the thin cloth. She reached behind to unhook the bra. It fell to the blanket.

JESSE MOANED at the sight of her round, full breasts dappled in sunlight. She stepped to him and pulled his shirt off. He hesitated only a moment before he drew her to him, skin to skin, wrapping his arms around her, holding her. He told himself this wasn't happening. He'd wanted it too badly. He could feel her heart, its emphatic beat keeping time with his own. He looked down at her. And wondered why she was giving herself to him.

Not for the reason he would have hoped, that much he knew. But did it matter?

She leaned up to kiss him, her kiss heated. She pulled away to shuck off the rest of her clothing, seemingly as anxious to make love to him as he was to her.

He watched her, enthralled, completely captivated as she stripped, then dove into the pool of water, droplets momentarily suspended in the air around her, her skin silky as the water that rippled over it.

"Are you joining me?" she called.

He took off his clothes, the ledger falling from his pocket onto the blanket. Then he followed her into the water.

The pool was waist deep, the water wonderfully cool, the bottom a fine sand. He moved to her, pulling her into his arms, feeling her nakedness against his own. He dropped his mouth to hers. Her lips parted, welcoming him, as her body pressed to his and he enveloped her, the way the water enveloped them both.

His kiss left her breathless, the taste of him on her lips, the scent of him branded in her memory. She watched as he cupped the cool water in his hands and poured it over her breasts, letting it run down her belly to her navel, to the golden V between her legs. His mouth followed the path of the water.

Then he swept her up in his arms and carried her to the blanket beside the river. He made love to her, slowly, deliberately, passionately. She opened to him, surrendering to his touch, giving herself to him in a way she knew she would never give to another man.

He took her to dizzying heights, and finally crying out, she reached the zenith with him. She clung to him, tears blurring her vision at the realization that she would never see Jesse again after tonight.

He left her sated, sensuously serene, his body lying next to hers, the air around them cooling as he drifted off, holding her in his arms.

She waited, listening to his soft, steady breathing, the sound of the sighing boughs overhead and the murmur of the river. Then she looked over on the blanket to where the ledger had fallen out of his pocket.

She felt the serenity evaporate the way the water had on her skin, the way the sweat from their love-making had. She checked her watch. Earlier, while Jesse had been in the old Duncan place, she'd called Gage. The trade was set for tonight at an old bridge outside of Dallas. She could take off now, hide out and make the trade. Without Jesse. Just as she'd planned.

Carefully, she slipped from his arms and crawled over to the ledger. In the shade of the tree, she opened the small bound pages, her father's handwriting filling her with conflicting emotions. Through her tears, she saw that handwriting on all the cards he'd given her over the years, all the presents with loving notes attached, all the checks signed to her, gifts he'd given from the heart. And in this book, she saw his other life, the illegal, dishonest, deceitful, horrible one. She'd known some of his business dealings were illegal. She just hadn't known the extent of it.

She closed the book and sat looking down at it, remembering her plan to take the ledger and leave without Jesse, her plan to do this alone. Then she looked over at him. He was still sleeping, his dark eyes closed, his chest rising and falling. She felt a catch in her throat—in her heart. She thought of the little baby left beside the road. Of the man who'd saved her life last night. Of their lovemaking.

She couldn't fall for a cop. Let alone a Kincaid. Could she?

With a silent curse, she put the ledger back where she'd found it and, fighting the urge to curl up again in his arms, headed for the river to bathe before they had to leave.

JESSE OPENED one eye and watched her. He smiled to himself as he saw her change her mind and put the ledger back and walk into the cool water of the river. He had never seen a more beautiful woman. His heart convulsed at the sight of her, at her trust in him. They would make the trade together. But then she would take Susannah and leave the country. He'd lied to himself, believing making love to her once would be enough. Not one time, one day or one lifetime would be enough of this woman.

He watched her glide through the water, her naked body glistening in the sunlight, then he rose and followed her into the river. They still had a little time before they had to leave.

Chapter Thirteen

The sun left the sky infused with color as it sank into the horizon. Amanda changed the plates on the van from Texas plates to the Louisiana ones she had in the back. She stuck a couple of bumper stickers on the back: Proud to Be a Grandma and This Van Stops at Garage Sales, then she slapped up some gaudy stick-on blinds at the windows.

"Looks like a different van, doesn't it?" she said as she considered her handiwork. "I figured Sheriff Wilson called in the plates. Anyone looking for us will be searching for a tan van with Texas plates."

Jesse had to agree the van looked entirely different.

"Who do you think is looking for us?" he asked.

She shrugged. "Maybe no one. But there's no reason to take a chance. Not when I'm this close to making the trade for my daughter."

Jesse didn't buy it. He wondered who had her worried. Probably her father. Maybe Gage. Or whoever owned that dark car with the knocking engine.

"At least I know the van is clean," she said. "I checked it myself for tracking devices before we left Dallas." She produced a small box from the glove compartment. "This detects any kind of bug or foreign electronic device, including a G.P.S."

He nodded and smiled. "Electrical engineering, huh?"

She shrugged. "I always liked gadgets. I rewired the intercom in the house when I was a teenager so my father couldn't spy on me. Getting around Daddy's expensive security system is child's play."

He doubted that.

On the edge of Dallas, he glanced in his rear-view mirror, something he'd done so many times without incident that he almost dismissed the car coming up fast behind them.

"Get down!" he ordered, reaching for Amanda before going for the gun at his waist.

He pushed her to the floorboard as a dark-colored, expensive car closed the distance between them.

"Who is it?" she asked, her voice cracking.

He could see the tear in her eyes and knew she was worried that J.B.'s goons would find her and keep her from making the trade. "I don't know yet."

Jesse flipped up the rearview mirror and leaned back so his reflection couldn't be seen in the side mirror, either. "Just stay down." The car looked familiar. He laid the gun on his thigh, being careful to keep his speed the same.

The car following him swung out into the passing lane, then sped by as if Jesse were standing still. Jesse sat back as it zoomed past. There were at least three guys in the car.

"They're gone," he said and looked over. Amanda had moved to the back of the van and must have been looking out the tinted side window.

"I recognized one of them," she said as she climbed back into the front seat.

"One of Mickie Ferraro's men, right?" He'd heard the engine's distinctive knock as the car sped past. "It was the same vehicle that tried to run you down just last night in Dallas."

She stared at him. "Why?"

"For the ledger, I would imagine."

"But how— I know what you're thinking. Gage wouldn't—"

"The hell he wouldn't," Jesse snapped. "Who else knew about the trade?"

"The kidnapper."

"You really don't believe Mickie Ferraro is working with the Governor now?" he asked.

She fell silent. "It can't be Gage. He's determined to make the trade."

"But he doesn't need you. In fact, if you were dead, he would get Susannah, right?"

"He'd have to fight my father," she said. "There would be bloodshed but—" She seemed to hesitate. "It *would* put Mickie right where he wants to be with the Organization."

Jesse's head snapped around as he looked over at her, his eyes widening. "If something happened to you, your father would go to war with whoever he thought was behind your murder, right?"

She nodded.

"But wouldn't he suspect Kincaid rather than Mickie Ferraro?"

She seemed to pale. "You're worried about the trade tonight, aren't you?"

"Damned right, I am. I've been worried since the cops showed up at the last one. Dirty cops, I'd wager. Except I don't believe they were your father's."

"What can we do?" she asked quietly.

We. Making love to Amanda had done nothing to exorcize the desire he'd felt for her. Instead, the desire had become a force to be reckoned with as if it had taken on a life of its own. He wanted more than ever to be her gallant knight and slay all her dragons. Especially that big, ugly one, Gage Ferraro and his hoodlum father.

He watched the road ahead, still worried that the car with the men might be waiting for them.

"I think Gage is too smart to try to pull something like that again," she said. "He wants the ledger too badly."

And why was that, Jesse wondered. To save his daughter? That didn't sound like the Gage Ferraro he knew. Nor did Jesse believe Gage was trying to get into J. B. Crowe's good graces. What *was* going on?

Whatever it was, Amanda and her baby's life hung in the balance.

He found a side road, one that would skirt around Dallas, and took it.

"Where are we going?" Amanda asked.

"I have to talk to Kincaid," he said, knowing she wasn't going to like it.

"Kincaid? You have to be kidding. Do you really think he'll even let you in the door?"

"I think he will, once he sees me," Jesse said. "I have a feeling I resemble my father."

"What makes you think that?" she asked.

"Your father's initial reaction to me," he said. "I misunderstood it that day I first met him."

"I assume my near accident was a setup?" she asked.

He didn't like the edge to her voice. "I'm a cop."

"So all is fair in the fight of good to overcome evil?" she asked.

He shot her a look, realizing that the lines had blurred considerably for him over the last few days. "I won't apologize for trying to bring down your father, but I was wrong to paint you with the same dirty brush." He reached for her hand and squeezed it. "If you don't want to see Kincaid—"

"No," she said. "I do." Her voice broke. "I want to make a plea for my baby."

"What if he didn't take her?" Jesse had to ask.

She said nothing, just stared out the windshield, as he drove south to Austin and the capitol.

IT TOOK SEVERAL phone calls to find the governor once they reached Austin, then the person who answered the call refused to put Jesse through.

"Tell the governor it's about a close relative of his," Jesse said. A few moments later, Governor Thomas Kincaid came on the line. Jesse was sure the call was being traced.

"Yes?" Kincaid said, sounding old and tired and scared.

"I need to talk to you in person," Jesse said.

"What is this about?" Kincaid asked.

"You'll know when you see me," Jesse said.

Kincaid didn't hesitate long. "You know where I live?"

Everyone knew where the governor's mansion was. "I'm just around the corner. I can be there in two minutes. I think it's best if we come in through the back."

"We?" Kincaid asked.

Jesse felt an arrow of guilt pierce his heart. Kincaid thought this was about his daughter Diana. "Two minutes." He hung up and looked at Amanda. She looked scared. She still believed that Kincaid was behind the kidnapping of her daughter. She must feel as if they were going into the lion's den.

He took her hand. "We're in."

She gave him a tentative smile. "I hope you're right about this."

"Me, too," he said. "But I'll get us back out of there if I'm not. One way or another."

KINCAID MET THEM at the back door, just as Jesse figured he would. Several "suits" stood in the shadows, obviously armed.

The governor looked as if he hadn't slept for days. Jesse knew he probably hadn't. The older man's gaze went first to Amanda, his eyes widening in surprise. Then he looked at Jesse. For a moment Jesse thought he might faint.

"Can we come in?" Jesse said. "We need to talk to you."

Kincaid stumbled back, motioning to the men that everything was fine, when Jesse knew it wasn't. All the color had gone out of the governor's face and his hand trembled as he opened a door and ushered them into what appeared to be a TV room, furnished with comfortable chairs and a large-screen television.

"Who are you?" Kincaid asked dropping into a chair, his gaze never leaving Jesse's face.

Jesse sat down next to Amanda on the love seat. He took her hand. Now that he was here, he didn't know where to begin. But Kincaid's reaction resolved any questions he might have had about his resemblance to his father.

"I believe I'm your nephew," he said. "Billy's son."

Kincaid leaned back in his chair and glanced at Amanda, distrust in his expression.

"Let me explain," Jesse said, realizing he had to lay all of his cards on the table. "My name is Jesse McCall. I'm a cop. An undercover cop. I've been working as J. B. Crowe's chauffeur the last couple of weeks." He filled Kincaid in on everything, including what he'd learned in Red River.

Kincaid shook his head as if in shock. "I'll admit the resemblance is uncanny but—"

Jesse pulled the gold heart from his jeans pocket

and held it out to the governor. The older man's reaction erased any doubt.

"Oh, my God," Kincaid said, tears filling his eyes.

"My adoptive parents found this heart in my baby blanket," Jesse said. "I need to know who my mother is. I need to know what happened and how I ended up beside that dirt road."

"I didn't know she was pregnant. Billy never told me. But I did know how he felt about her. I never met her. Billy and I...well we were at odds over his involvement with—" He glanced toward Amanda.

"Billy and my father were best friends," she said haughtily. "Billy's death changed my father's life."

Kincaid nodded, no doubt thinking how his little brother's death had changed his, as well. He looked to Jesse. "If I had known about you, I wouldn't have let anything happen to you."

Jesse believed him. "What was my mother's name?"

"Roxie. Roxie Pickett."

"Is she still alive?" Jesse asked.

Kincaid shook his head. "She died two days after my brother. She killed herself."

Jesse felt as if the floor had fallen out from under him. For a moment he couldn't speak. "Her parents?"

"I think they still live in the old neighborhood," Kincaid said, his tone implying it was the same one where he and Billy and J.B. were raised. "I think the father's name was Frank. Frank Pickett. It's been so long. I can't remember the wife's name."

Kincaid stared at him, obviously in shock. "You look so much like Billy." He looked ill, not powerful, not frightening.

Jesse could see that Amanda had lost some of the anger in her expression. She just looked scared for her baby.

"I need to ask you about another child," Jesse said. "Susannah Crowe, Amanda's six-month-old baby."

Kincaid's gaze flicked to Amanda. "Your daughter is missing?"

"I wouldn't think that comes as a surprise."

Kincaid looked back to Jesse. "It does make things clearer though."

Jesse nodded. "Like her father, Amanda believes you're behind the kidnapping because the kidnapper is demanding evidence against J. B. Crowe."

Kincaid closed his eyes for a moment. When he opened them, they swam in tears. "I understand your frustration, Ms. Crowe. My daughter and her unborn baby are also missing. But I did not have your baby kidnapped. I wish there was some way

I could make you believe that. Make your father believe that, if it is not too late for my daughter. I pray it is not too late for your daughter, as well.''

Amanda stared at him, looking numb.

Jesse couldn't tell if she believed the governor or not. It didn't matter really what any of them believed. ''I plan to find out who kidnapped Susannah Crowe,'' Jesse warned Kincaid. ''If you're involved I will bring you down no matter who you are.''

Kincaid nodded solemnly.

Jesse and Amanda rose. Kincaid pushed himself to his feet. He seemed awkward as if he didn't know what to say but didn't want Jesse to leave either. He held out his hand. Jesse shook it, feeling a strength that assured him his uncle would be fine. His uncle. That would take some getting used to.

''Will I see you again?'' Kincaid said.

''Yes.'' Jesse followed Amanda to the door. ''When this is all over, we'll both come back.''

FRANK AND MOLLY Pickett lived in a neighborhood of Dallas that had seen better days. Rustedout cars balanced wheelless on blocks, garbage cluttered the gutters and graffiti defiled the faces of the weathered buildings.

Amanda tried to imagine her father growing up here, let alone Kincaid. She shivered at the thought of the children who still grew up here and thought of Kincaid's programs to replace these neighborhoods with homes for the poor. She'd always thought his plan was political. Now she wasn't so sure.

"The van probably won't be here when we get back," Amanda noted as Jesse parked in front of the address he'd found in the phone book.

"Do you have some money?" he asked her. "A twenty and a fifty?"

She gave him a questioning look, but dug out the bills and handed them to him, then climbed out of the van after him.

Jesse approached one of the young men sitting on a stoop in the shade. "See this twenty?" he said to the man. "I have a fifty for you as well if I come back and that van hasn't been touched. It's better than what you're going to get from the guys who steal or strip these cars."

The man smiled at that and took the twenty. "Don't be long."

Amanda knew Jesse had no intention of being any longer than necessary. She could feel his tension when he put his hand on her back and led her up the stairs. She felt uneasy and knew it wasn't just the neighborhood that was making her feel that way.

Jesse rang the buzzer on the apartment marked Pickett. The sun beat down in waves of heat while a putrid stench rose from the rainwater and garbage lying stagnant in the gutter.

"Yes?" came an older female voice.

"Mrs. Pickett?" Jesse asked.

"Yes?" came the hesitant answer.

He looked at Amanda as if he didn't know what to say.

"We're friends of the family and just wanted to stop by," Amanda said into the speaker.

Silence. Then the crackle of the speaker. "Come on up, then," the woman said and buzzed them in.

Jesse shot her a look of gratitude and Amanda smiled, wanting to touch his face, hold him in her arms. She'd never felt like this about a man before. Safe. Protected. Cared for. And yet part of her held back, afraid. Afraid of the future. Some things were just too good to be true. And Jesse McCall was one of them.

At 2A, Jesse knocked. Inside the apartment came the sound of a radio. Jesse knocked again.

The door swung open. A small, white-haired woman appeared wiping her hands on the apron she wore. The apron was a bright, multicolored fruit pattern and each time she wiped her hands, she left a white flour handprint on the cloth.

"Sorry, I didn't hear your knock," she said and smiled cheerfully as she pushed open the door. "Come on in. I was just baking a pie." She turned on her heel and led them inside.

Amanda shot Jesse a look, taken aback by the woman's friendliness as they followed her into the kitchen.

"It's going to be a scorcher," the woman commented as they trailed her into the large homey kitchen where she picked up the rolling pin she had discarded and began to work at the golden dough on the floured board. The room felt warm and smelled of apples. "And it's only spring."

The apartment was surprisingly nice inside with a feeling that the people who lived here had no intention of ever moving again.

Amanda had never lived in a home like this. It tugged at something deep inside her. She spotted a photograph on the top of a buffet and glanced over at Jesse.

JESSE HAD SEEN the photo the moment he walked into the room. It was a young girl. He wondered if it was Roxie Pickett or some other little girl, maybe a sister.

"We're sorry to bother you—" Jesse began.

"Oh, it's no bother at all." The elderly woman looked up then, meeting his gaze. "You say you're a friend of the family?"

He'd hoped, he realized, that she would recognize him. She didn't seem to. "Possibly even a distant relative. That's why we're here. To find out."

Molly seemed fine with that. "Everyone just calls me Molly," she said. "Nice to have a little company. Hardly ever see anyone. I'm sorry I don't have the pie done or I would offer you a piece."

"That isn't necessary," Jesse managed to say. "But it is a nice offer."

For a moment, he watched her work the crust, rolling it with practiced expertise until it was thin and smooth, the edges round. He had so many questions, he didn't know where to begin.

"I need to ask you about your side of the family," he said.

She smiled. "I'll tell you what I can."

He took a breath. "You're married to Frank Pickett, right?"

She nodded. "Have been for more than forty years," she said proudly.

"And your children?" he asked and immediately regretted it.

Her face clouded over for a moment, then cleared. "Had one daughter, but she died. Just had the one."

"And her name was Roxie?"

Molly looked up and appeared surprised. "That's right. Roxanna Lynn but everyone called her Roxie."

Jesse felt his heart pounding. "I suppose you have some pictures of her?"

Molly studied him as she wiped her hands again on her apron. "You want to see her?"

"Very much so," he said.

She seemed to hesitate, but only for a moment. "I have a photo of her on the buffet, but some more recent ones are in here." Jesse and Amanda followed the woman into a bedroom. "This was taken not long before—" she looked up "—when she was sixteen."

Jesse took the photograph in the tarnished frame and felt his heart hammer against his ribs. His mother. She took his breath way. Beautiful dark eyes, long dark hair. The face of an angel. Tears filled his eyes.

Noticing his reaction, Molly took the framed photo from him. "Will you tell me what this is about?" she asked, her voice sounding weak, scared.

His throat seemed to close. All he could do was stare at the other photographs on the wall. Many of Roxie. One when she was about eleven, standing holding up a fish for the camera, her eyes bright, a smile on her face.

Amanda saved him. "Mrs. Pickett—"

"Molly."

"Molly, your daughter had a baby just before she died," Amanda said.

Molly's gaze swung to Amanda's, but she said nothing.

"We need to know about the baby," Amanda said.

"There is nothing to tell," Molly said. "The baby died."

Fishing. Jesse realized most all of the photographs on the wall were of fish. Roxie at varying ages. Alone and with a man, a man who looked like her. Roxie's father. Frank Pickett. Jesse stepped closer to study the man in the snapshot, asking himself what he'd come here for. He knew now who his birth parents had been. Even his grandfather, he thought studying the picture.

Jesse only half listened to Amanda trying to talk to Molly about the baby as he dragged his gaze from the man's face to the cabin behind him and the weathered sign over the cabin door. He was trying to read the words, when something else drew his attention. Off to his right was a photograph of Roxie in her teens. Around her neck she wore a gold chain. The unusual heart dangled from the end.

"We know the baby didn't die," he heard Amanda say and turned his attention back to the room and the elderly woman wringing her hands in her apron.

Molly dropped into a chair. "You're wrong. The baby was born dead." She began to cry. "Frank was there. He said it was God's will, a baby conceived in sin, by a man like that."

"A man like that? You knew the father then? The man she was dating?"

Molly shook her head looking confused. "Roxie was only sixteen. She wasn't allowed to date. She met him secretly. Frank saw the heart around her neck—" She began to cry again. "He found out who'd had the heart made, then he knew who the father was, the father of this child born before its time."

"The baby came early?" Amanda asked in surprise. "Then the baby was born here in the house?"

Molly shook her head. "At Roxie's friend's next door." She got to her feet. "I have to finish dinner. My husband will be home from fishing soon. None of this matters anymore."

"I'm that baby," Jesse said, finally finding the words.

Molly swung around to face him, her eyes wide. Slowly she lowered herself into a chair again. "That isn't possible."

"I'm afraid it is," he said. Couldn't she see her daughter in him? Something around the eyes? He reached into his pocket and withdrew the heart. He held it out to her.

Molly gasped and put her hands over her mouth, her eyes huge above her fingers.

"The night he was born, someone wrapped him in a blanket and put him in a cardboard box,"

Amanda said, kneeling before the woman. "Roxie had just enough time to write a note and put it and the heart into the baby blanket. Then someone took the child away and left him in the box beside a dirt road north of here near Red River. Only, he was found before he could die."

Molly seemed to be gasping for breath. "Please go," she whimpered. "I don't want you upsetting my husband with all this."

"Let's go," Jesse said and took Amanda's arm to help her to her feet. "She doesn't want to hear this. And it doesn't matter who left me there. I found out what I needed to know."

"But Jesse—"

"Please," he said meeting Amanda's gaze. "Let's just get out of here."

She nodded, tears in her eyes. For a woman who didn't care about justice, she'd certainly tried hard to at least get at the truth for him.

He wanted to take her in his arms and hold her and thank her and make love to her again. And again. She was in his system now and he wondered how he could ever get her out. If he could bear to even try.

As he and Amanda came out of the apartment, Jesse felt numb. He'd gotten what he'd come for. Almost. He still didn't know who had left him beside the road. But what did it matter really? Maybe whoever had delivered him really did believe he was dead. Or maybe not.

He put his arm around Amanda as they descended the steps into the hot, horrible-smelling street. They'd found one baby. Now they had to find hers. Jesse promised himself that he could at least give Amanda the justice she deserved. He would get her daughter back and bring the kidnapper in. No matter who he was.

The van was still there. The young man was sitting guard on the steps halfway down. He didn't say a word, just held out his hand. Jesse put the fifty into his open palm as he and Amanda passed.

The feeling came out of the blue. That distinct prickle at the back of his neck. His feet had just touched the sidewalk, when he heard the screech of tires and a familiar engine knock.

''Get down!'' he yelled as he dragged Amanda to the concrete behind the van. The sound of gunfire echoed off the buildings as the car sped past.

Jesse got off two shots. One took out the back window of the dark-green car. The other made a hollow sound as it pierced the trunk lid. Behind him, he heard the young man on the steps take off at a dead run.

Chapter Fourteen

Amanda rose slowly from the ground. "That was Mickie's men again, wasn't it?"

"Yes," Jesse agreed, opening the van door. The side of the van was riddled with holes. "Get in and stay down."

She slid in with him close behind.

He started the van and flipped around to go in the opposite direction. "They have some way of tracking us. It's the only thing that makes sense. Sheriff Wilson might have called in the plates on the van, alerting those cops who tried to arrest us the other night. Somehow they got to this van."

He drove a few miles, then pulled over. "You have a way of checking for a bug, right?"

She nodded, opened the glove box and pulled out her gear. She found the bug within a few minutes. "Someone would have had to put it on while we were in the Corral Bar talking to Huey. I should have checked the van again."

She tore the bug from the under carriage of the van and smashed it, then climbed back in. Suddenly a thought hit her. "What if Mickie Ferraro has a very good reason for not wanting me to make the trade?" she asked when Jesse got back in.

He glanced over at her. "The ledger. You think there is something in there that incriminates him as well as your father?"

Her heart began to beat a little faster. "There has to be. But how does Mickie know about the ledger and the trade?"

"Those cops who tried to bust us last night," Jesse said. "They might work for Gage. Or they might also be on Mickie's payroll if the money is right. One of them could have spilled the beans about a ledger they were supposed to get from you—and where."

That would explain how Mickie's men had found her and almost run her down. "You don't think Gage—"

"Is hoping to get rid of both J.B. and his father and take over their territory?" Jesse asked sarcastically.

She leaned back in her seat, trying to figure all of the angles as Jesse drove toward the old Ballantine Bridge and the trade with the kidnapper.

"The only way it makes sense is if Kincaid is behind the kidnapping," she pointed out. "Kincaid could bust my father and Mickie and clear the way for Gage.''

''Unless Gage is behind the kidnapping,'' Jesse said quietly.

She looked over at him, her heart pounding. Better than anyone, she knew what Gage was capable of. But not the kidnapping of his own child.

''He might want the ledger as insurance,'' Jesse said. ''With it, he would control both J.B. and his father.''

That was one possibility she didn't want to even consider. She would rather have believed Kincaid was behind the kidnapping. But she had to admit he'd confused her earlier when they'd talked to him. He didn't seem the kind of man who could kidnap an infant, but then her father didn't seem like the kind of man who could steal babies and sell them in the black market, either.

She tried not to think of Susannah. Or babies left in cardboard boxes beside dirt roads or sold on the black market. She'd convinced herself that Susannah's kidnapper would take good care of her daughter. That any kidnapper who took J. B. Crowe's granddaughter knew better than to harm the child.

But at the same time, she couldn't imagine any one arrogant enough to mess with her mobster father and his family. That was another reason she was convinced the kidnapper had to be Kincaid. As governor, Kincaid might feel bulletproof.

But Gage had been furious at being exiled to Chicago. And equally furious with her.

Gage could be behind Susannah's kidnapping as much as she didn't want to believe it.

"You might be right," she said. "We might be dealing with Gage."

"Better than Mickie and friends. We're almost to the bridge."

"I'm frightened, Jesse," she admitted.

He smiled over at her, reaching out to cup her cheek in his hand. "Don't worry, I have a plan."

Now more than ever, he was convinced Gage had to be behind the kidnapping. It was the only thing that made any sense.

He drove toward the old bridge, anything but calm about the trade. Amanda had repeated the instructions Gage had given her earlier. Jesse had little option but to follow them.

It was her daughter's life at risk. He would do everything he could to protect her and Susannah, but without police backup. Alone. He had no other choice. He'd be afraid to involve the police even if she'd have let him. He no longer knew who he could trust.

And he desperately wanted the kidnapper. Wanted to nail the bastard. No matter what Amanda said about not caring if the man was brought to justice. Would she change her mind if the man was Gage Ferraro?

He looked over at her, wishing there was something more to say. It didn't help the ache in his chest at just the sight of her.

The Trinity River was running full from spring runoff. Water rushed between its banks, dark waves hurling tree limbs and debris downstream.

Ballantine Bridge was an old county bridge about twenty miles out of Dallas, a long span of steel covered with rotting boards over the Trinity River. The bridge had been closed to the public for years. A metal crossbar over each end allowed only pedestrian traffic—mostly fishermen.

Jesse stopped a good mile from the bridge, pulling the van off the road into a stand of dense trees. He could see the river through the branches, the water brown with silt and moving fast. He took one of the weapons, checked the clip on the other and handed it to her.

She stared down at the gun. "I'm not going to need this."

"Better safe than sorry. Put it in the waistband of your jeans in the back. Your jacket will cover it."

"I told you, Jesse, I don't care about the kidnapper," she repeated. "I just want my daughter."

"That's what I want too, sweetheart," he assured her. "But sometimes things go wrong."

"Nothing better go wrong."

He nodded at her warning and handed her the ledger from his jacket pocket.

She took it, her hands trembling.

"If it came down to catching the kidnapper or saving Susannah, you know I would let the kidnapper get away, don't you?" he asked.

She looked into his eyes and nodded, then leaned over to kiss his lips. He pulled her to him, holding her tightly as he deepened the kiss, overpowered by the taste and feel of her. A live wire of desire shot through him. Lord, how he wanted her. Reluctantly, he let her go.

"We'll get your baby back," he said to her, his palm cupping her cheek.

She nodded, tears in her eyes. "I know."

He wanted to tell her what he was feeling, but he couldn't even put it into coherent thoughts for himself, let alone words for her.

"Jesse—" She seemed to stop herself. "Be careful."

He nodded. "You, too. I'll be there when you need me." But even as he said the words, he knew that wouldn't always be true. He was a cop. She was a mobster's daughter. Once Amanda got her daughter back, she planned to skip the country. Jesse had no intention of spending the rest of his life on the run. After tonight, it would be over between them.

His heart ached at the mere thought, but he only had himself to blame. He'd done the worst thing he could have: he'd made love to her. And now the memory of their lovemaking would haunt him forever. He couldn't imagine the day he wouldn't want her, wouldn't remember her scent or the feel of her skin.

He climbed out of the van, stuffed the weapon into his waistband and waited for her to slide behind the wheel before he closed the door. "Give me twenty minutes."

She nodded, and he turned and hurried off into the woods, telling himself that the next time he saw her, she would have her baby back.

AMANDA WAITED, counting off the minutes with the steady thump of her heart. Finally she would get to see her daughter. To hold her baby in her arms again. To put all of this behind them.

But she didn't kid herself. She knew she would also be putting Jesse behind her. He wouldn't be going with her and Susannah. It shocked her how much that realization hurt. She had fallen so hard, so fast for a man who was all wrong for her. A cop. It was almost laughable. She couldn't have done worse. Even Gage would have been preferable in the world she'd grown up in.

But Jesse McCall was exactly the kind of man she wanted as a father for Susannah. Exactly the kind of man she'd dreamed of for herself, although she'd never imagined that such passion could exist between two people. Nor did she kid herself that she could ever find a man like Jesse or that kind of passion again.

The waiting was torture. When twenty minutes had gone by, she started the van and drove down the narrow gravel road. The river ran entwined in the trees off to her left. She followed it, approaching the bridge slowly, her heart in her throat. A half-dozen fears clouded her thoughts, fears for Susannah. Fears for Jesse. She couldn't bear the thought of losing either of them. But then she reminded herself, Jesse wasn't hers to lose.

The bridge glittered dully in the dying light. Dust settled deep and dark along the river's edge. Tree limbs drooped into the rushing water, pockets of darkness pooled beneath them as the daylight slipped away.

She brought the van to a stop just before the bridge, just as she'd been instructed, turned off the engine and climbed out. Across the expanse of steel and rotting timbers, she could see another vehicle parked on the other side. The car door opened. A man stepped out. He held a bundle in his arms.

She felt her heart leap. It took everything in her not to run across the bridge to him and rip her child from his arms. She listened intently for the sound of her baby, cooing, even crying. Any indication that Susannah was finally within reach.

But she heard nothing over the sound of the water surging under the bridge as she ducked under the barricade and started across. On the other side, the man did the same. They were to meet in the middle and make the exchange. She gripped the ledger in her hand and walked toward him.

As she grew closer, she could make out his features. She wasn't surprised that she didn't recognize him. Kincaid would use someone she didn't know. So would Gage. Not that it mattered now who'd kidnapped Susannah. Just as long as Amanda got her baby back, safe and sound.

But as she walked across the old bridge, the boards making a hollow sound beneath her soles, something cold and hard settled in her stomach, a fear she couldn't shake off. What if she was wrong? What if the person who had her baby wasn't going to give Susannah up easily?

She didn't dare look around for Jesse. She didn't dare stop walking. She could feel the gun digging into her back but she knew she wouldn't draw it, wouldn't fire it. Even though she'd learned to shoot, she'd never used a weapon against anything more than a paper outline of a man.

She was almost to the man when he stopped.

"Where is the ledger?" he called out to her.

She held it up for him to see.

"Lay it down and back up," he ordered. "I'll take it and leave the baby."

"No," she said, surprising him and herself. "We make the trade, eye to eye."

He shook his head. "No. You want the baby? Then you do it my way."

She took a breath. Susannah was so close, so close. She swallowed. What choice did she have but to trust him? She'd come this far. "All right." Hands shaking, she put the ledger down on the wooden boards that spanned across the bridge supports. Through a crack, she could see the river raging far below her. She felt dizzy and sick to her stomach with fear.

Slowly she backed up, one step at a time. The man waited until she had retreated a good distance before he advanced. She felt her heart thundering in her chest, her pulse so loud she couldn't hear the river anymore.

He approached the ledger lying on the boards, appearing wary. Carefully, he put the baby down, scooped up the ledger, took a quick look inside, then turned his back and began to walk quickly back to his car.

She could wait no longer. She took off at a run, tears blinding her, a cry in her throat as she rushed to her baby daughter.

JESSE SLOWLY approached the vehicle on the far side of the river. He could see a man hunched down in the seat, hiding, waiting. For what? He had watched the first man cross the bridge to meet Amanda, carrying the baby in his arms, and waited, not about to do anything until Amanda had Susannah and the two were safe.

Once the man put down the baby and moved away, Jesse knew he had only a few seconds to get to the second man in the vehicle before the first man started back. If he could disable the man in the car, it would even the odds and keep the men from possibly reneging on the trade.

It bothered Jesse that the first man had taken no precaution to keep from being recognized in a police line-up. Were they so sure that Amanda would never press charges? Or were they planning never to give her the chance?

The moment the man surrendered the baby, Jesse moved quickly up the right side of the car. His hand had just closed over the door handle when he heard Amanda scream, a blood-chilling scream that set his heart pumping.

The man in the car sat up with a jerk and threw open his door. Jesse barely got out of the way before the man leapt from the car. Jesse recognized him instantly. Gage Ferraro.

Gage didn't even see Jesse behind him. All of his attention was on the bridge. Before Jesse could

react, Gage took off running toward the first man—
and Amanda.

With a curse, Jesse went after him, his heart in
his throat. Was something wrong with the baby?
Oh, dear God, don't let Susannah be dead.

Gage didn't seem to hear Jesse behind him over
the rush of the water. Amanda had dropped to her
knees in the middle of the bridge. The baby
seemed to roll out of her arms. Her scream still
echoed off the steel girders.

The first man was running hard back toward
Gage and the car, the ledger in his hand. Jesse
watched in horror as Amanda straightened and
reached behind her.

The shot reverberated across the river. The man
with the ledger jerked, stumbled and fell face first
onto the bridge.

For a moment, Jesse thought she'd shoot Gage
as well, but she lowered the gun as he ran toward
her as if she thought he was running to her. If she
did, she was dead wrong.

Gage rushed to the downed man, grabbed the
ledger from the dead man's hand and turned
around, already moving back toward Jesse before
he saw him.

The look on Gage's face gave him away as
much as his actions. Jesse saw Gage go for his gun.
Jesse hadn't even realized it, but he already had
his weapon in his hand. Amanda was still on her

knees, out of his line of fire. He raised his gun, almost in slow motion and squeezed off a shot, then another. He could hear Amanda scream, "No!" A shot whizzed by Jesse's left ear and pinged off the steel girders.

Gage lost his grip on his gun as he fell. The weapon hit the worn boards of the bridge before Gage did and skittered off, dropping over the side into the river.

Gage was trying to get up as Jesse ran to him.

"Don't kill him!" Amanda was screaming. She'd gotten to her feet and had run toward them. She still had the gun in her hand and what at first looked like a baby dangling from the other. But as she drew closer, Jesse saw that it was a doll. Not Susannah, but a doll.

Jesse jerked Gage up to a sitting position. Gage had taken a bullet in his side; he'd survive. The second shot had grazed his arm. "Where is Susannah?" Jesse demanded.

Gage shook his head. "I know my rights," he said recognizing Jesse for the cop who'd sent him up on the drug charge a few years ago. "I don't have to tell you anything."

"*I'm* not a cop," Amanda said behind Jesse. The quiet calm in her voice made him turn. She stood over Gage, the gun in her hand, the barrel pointed at Gage's chest. "Where is my daughter?"

"Our daughter," he growled.

The shot was deafening and too close for comfort. Jesse jumped back.

"The next one will be in you," Amanda said quietly.

Gage swore. "You can't let her do this," he cried to Jesse. "You're a cop. Tell her, I have my rights."

Amanda got off a second shot before Jesse could get to her. Gage let out a howl and grabbed for his knee. Blood spurted through the neat round hole in his pants.

"Where is my daughter?" she asked again, a deadly calm in her voice. Her eyes were glazed over. She appeared to be in shock.

"All right," Gage groaned.

Jesse reached for Amanda's gun but stopped as Gage began to talk.

"I don't know anything about Susannah," Gage said. "I just had to have the ledger." He was crying now, holding his knee. "It was the cops. They got me on drug trafficking. We're talking the Big House. I had to do what they told me to."

"You made a deal, your neck for Crowe's *and* your father's?" Jesse asked in disbelief. "For... what?"

"A lighter sentence," Gage said. "Maybe even minimum security."

"You never had Susannah?" Amanda whispered.

"When I heard through my sources in the Organization that Susannah had been kidnapped, I didn't know of any other way to get you to deliver something big on your father," Gage said between sobs. "I knew you'd do it for Susannah. So I pretended I'd been contacted by the kidnapper and that the ledger was the ransom."

"After everything *else* you did to me?" Amanda asked.

Jesse had forgotten about the gun in Amanda's hand until she raised it and aimed point-blank at Gage's chest.

"No, Amanda!" Jesse shouted as he grabbed for her. As much as he despised Gage Ferraro for what he'd done, Jesse was still a cop. He still believed in playing by the rules. No matter how hard they were to abide by at times like this.

But as he grabbed for Amanda's gun, he made a fatal error. He diverted his attention from Gage for just a split second. Gage kicked his feet out from under him, knocking the gun from his hands and sending Amanda's weapon into the river.

Jesse came down hard, then Gage was on him, wrestling for Jesse's dropped weapon, and at the same time trying desperately to hang on to the ledger.

Jesse got a grip on the gun as they rolled dangerously close to the edge of the bridge where no railing would prevent them from dropping to the raging river below. Jesse's head and shoulders hung over the edge of the rotted timbers. Gage banged Jesse's hand with the weapon in it on one of the bridge's steel guy wires and tried to force him over the edge.

With everything going against him, Jesse felt the gun slip from his grasp and knew he'd be dropping to the river next. He could see Amanda out of the corner of his eye. She'd run down the bridge a few yards and picked up what appeared to be a piece of pipe. She was running back toward them, but Jesse knew she wasn't going to make it in time. He felt the rotten edge of the timber give a little more under him.

He could grab for a guy wire as he fell—or the ledger. He grabbed for the ledger, knocking it loose from Gage's grasp. The ledger skidded across the wood along the edge of the bridge, headed for the river.

Gage let out a howl and dove for it, coming down hard on the rotted timbers. As Jesse grabbed the guy wires and pulled himself back onto the bridge, he heard the timber give way next to him and saw Gage fall.

Jesse scrambled to his feet and rushed over to where Gage had dropped over the edge. Gage had managed to grab hold of one of the girders with his free hand as he went over. He now dangled by one arm, his prize, the ledger, in the other hand.

"Let go of the ledger," Jesse called to him as he laid on his belly and reached down to take Gage's hand. He could see that Gage's fingers were slipping on the rusted metal. "Drop the ledger and give me your hand!"

Gage's pupils were huge. He glanced down at the roaring river far below him, then up at Jesse. With great reluctance, he released the ledger. It fluttered down like a dried leaf to the water below.

Gage started to lift his free hand toward Jesse's but it was too late. His hold on the metal gave. He fell, his scream finally drowned out as he disappeared like the ledger into the turbulent water.

Jesse let out a curse. As he got to his feet, he turned to look at Amanda. She stood staring over the edge after Gage, the piece of pipe in her hand, a look of shock still on her face.

"He never had Susannah," she said, her voice a whisper. "He never even knew where she was."

Jesse pulled her into his arms and hugged her tightly. "It's all right. We'll find her." But suddenly he felt numb with fear: why hadn't the real kidnapper demanded a ransom?

Chapter Fifteen

Jesse didn't know how long he stood on the bridge holding her. For a long time, she felt like a granite statue in his arms. Then she began to soften and tremble, then shake. The sobs rose as if coming from someplace deep inside her. He wrapped her in his arms and waited for the storm to pass, not knowing what else to do.

When she stopped crying, she quickly wiped her eyes and stepped from his arms. He saw the determination and strength come back into her.

"Amanda, something is wrong with all this," he said, when he was sure she was ready to hear it. "Why hasn't there been a request for a ransom?"

She stared at him in confusion, then shook her head. "I thought there had been. But if Gage was telling the truth…"

Jesse nodded. "Then there never was a ransom demand." Did that mean that whoever had taken

Susannah didn't want anything from the Crowes? Suddenly he felt the hair on the back of his neck stand straight up. A chill skittered across his skin. He shivered as if he'd stepped on a grave. Maybe he had.

"Amanda, remember what Molly said about Roxie's baby? About it being God's will, conceived in sin, the son of evil."

She nodded.

"Jesse, what are you saying?"

"Molly said Frank found out who the father was by tracking down the jeweler who made the hearts. *J.B.* had the hearts made. Wasn't that what you told me?"

"You think Frank thought J.B. was the father of Roxie's baby?"

He nodded. "Amanda, the man who grabbed your baby in the department store, could he have been Frank Pickett?"

She could only stare at him.

"It's a long shot," he told her as he quickly ushered her from the bridge toward the van. "If there was no ransom, no demand for money or favors or evidence, then why kidnap your daughter? Unless it was revenge. I know I'm probably crazy, but I think we'd better go talk to Molly Pickett again. Maybe we'll get lucky and her husband Frank will be home from fishing."

IT WAS DARK by the time they reached Molly Pickett's apartment. This time a half dozen men loitered on the front steps, but Jesse didn't offer them money as he shoved his way past, drawing Amanda in his wake.

Jesse laid on the buzzer, but no one answered. He tried the door. To his surprise and uneasiness, it wasn't locked. "Molly?" he called as he pushed the door open and stepped inside.

Only one light glowed in the living room, a small desk lamp next to the phone. Otherwise, the room was pitch-black. He snapped on the overhead living room light. "Molly?"

No sound. Moving slowly, he searched the small two-bedroom apartment. It was empty. Worse, it appeared Molly had left in a hurry. The crust for the pie she'd been making was still curled around the rolling pin where it had been earlier. The apples, all neatly sliced in the bowl, had turned dark gray.

He glanced at Amanda. She motioned to the desk lamp. In the circle of gold light, the phone book lay open, the phone next to it.

Amanda moved to the desk. Jesse followed her. The yellow pages were open to the *F*'s. Firewood. Fireworks. First Aid Supplies. Fish and Seafood. Fishing Consultants. Fishing—Resorts. Fishing—Tackle and Supplies.

"Wait a minute," Jesse said, remembering the

photo of Roxie and her father in front of a fishing lodge. He moved to the wall of photographs. Behind him, he heard Amanda pick up the phone, then the sound of the line being redialed. "I'm going to try the redial button," Amanda said. "Maybe Molly tried to call him after we left."

He found what he was looking for. The wooden sign over the cabin door with the words carved in it, Woodland Lake Resort. Behind him he heard the distant voice on the speaker phone say, "Good evening, Woodland Lake Resort."

"Woodland Lake," Jesse said with a curse as Amanda hung up the phone. "Red River is between here and the lake."

"Oh, my God, Jesse."

He nodded, that cold chill turning to ice as it moved like a glacier up his spine. "Frank Pickett. Molly said he was there at the birth. He must have been the one who left me beside the road."

"No wonder Molly was upset," Amanda gasped. "She really believed you were dead."

"Until I showed her the heart pendant."

"Oh, God. Jesse, she must have gone up to the lake when he didn't come home tonight. She thinks he has Susannah!"

"So do I."

They scrambled out of the building and down the steps to the van. Fortunately, all four tires were still attached as they leapt in. Jesse started the engine and popped the clutch, praying they could reach Woodland Lake in time, praying this wasn't just some wild-goose chase.

WOODLAND LAKE RESORT sat at the edge of the lake, a large old log lodge with boat docks, rooms and a restaurant. Amanda stayed in the van while Jesse ran in to ask how to get to Frank Pickett's cabin. She could only assume either Frank didn't have a phone at the cabin or he hadn't been answering it when Molly had called, so she'd called the resort looking for him.

Amanda sat perfectly still, trying to remain calm. She'd had such high hopes earlier on the bridge, now it was hard to hope at all. She was still shaken by finding the plastic doll wrapped in the baby blanket. How could Gage have done that to her?

She pushed him out of her mind and thought of Frank Pickett. She could understand greed. She'd grown up around it. But Frank hadn't asked for money.

She also had a good understanding of revenge. If Frank Pickett believed that J. B. Crowe had fathered his daughter's baby, he might blame J.B. for Roxie taking her life. An eye for an eye. A child for a child. After all, he'd left Jesse beside a dirt road to die.

But why not take *her*, J.B.'s child, if he wanted

an eye for an eye? She felt a chill, remembering what Consuela had said about history repeating itself. Someone had tried to kidnap her when she was a child but had failed. Oh, my God, could it have been Frank Pickett?

If that were true then why had he waited so long? Or had something happened to remind him? She thought of recent articles in the paper about her father. The announcement that he'd been chosen for that stupid humanitarian award had come out in the paper the day before Susannah's kidnapping.

Oh, dear God. Jesse could be right. Frank Pickett could have Susannah.

The thought poleaxed her. What in God's name had he done with Susannah, a baby born of mobsters' children?

Jesse startled her from her dark thoughts as he leapt back into the van. He turned down a small dirt lane bordered by thick-leafed trees, the headlights cutting a swath through the darkness.

"It's just up the road a half mile," he said. "I want you to stay in the van. If Susannah's there, I'll get her and bring her to you. Amanda, are you listening to me?"

He glanced over at her and must have recognized the look on her face. He swore.

"Don't try to stop me, Jesse," she said softly.

He swore again. "Then stay behind me and do as I say."

She nodded. He had to know by now that she would move heaven and earth to just hold her baby in her arms again.

JESSE STOPPED the van in the middle of the narrow lane, blocking the road should anyone try to leave the cabin. Through the trees, he could see a light in the distance. Quietly he opened the van door and slipped out, closing it silently behind him. Amanda did the same.

They made their way through the darkness of the woods, following the flickering light spilling from the cabin. As they drew closer, Jesse could hear voices. The only weapon he had was the piece of pipe he'd taken from Amanda on the bridge. It was stuck up the sleeve of his jacket.

He inched closer, Amanda right behind him. He could hear Molly's voice, a thin whine, and a deeper voice, raised in anger.

"Go around to the back, but don't go in until I tell you," he ordered.

She nodded, that look in her eyes that told him she would do whatever she had to do.

He swore under his breath as he watched her retreat along the side of the small cabin wall until she disappeared into the darkness.

Then carefully, he rose and peeked in the window. Through a crack in the blinds he could see Frank. The man was pacing back and forth. Behind him, Jesse saw something that made his heart leap. A baby. Susannah lay on the couch wedged between two pillows. Her tiny legs and arms flailed the air. Thank God, she was all right.

Molly sat in a chair opposite the couch, wringing her hands, talking softly to Frank.

Keeping low, Jesse moved to the front door, reached up and cautiously tried the knob. It turned in his hand. The door wasn't locked. He hoped to surprise Frank. Catch him off guard. And hoped that Frank didn't have a weapon in his hand at the time.

Rising, he quietly opened the door a crack. He could hear them now.

"Frank, please listen to me," Molly was saying.

"Everything's going to be all right now Molly," said the large man with graying dark hair. He stood over Susannah. "Someday little Roxie and I will go fishing together." Frank moved over by the baby and reached down to touch one perfect little hand. "My little Roxie."

Jesse would have gone in then but as Frank turned, Jesse saw the gun in the man's other hand.

"That's not Roxie," Molly said crying. "That's not your little girl."

Frank's face seemed to cloud. He jerked his hand back. "You're right. That's the spawn of that mobster. I thought I got rid of that baby." He sounded confused, near tears. "I thought I got rid of him."

"Oh, Frank," Molly wailed. "Please, let's take this baby back where you got it. Don't do this."

"It's too late, Molly," Frank said. "My Roxie killed herself because of that mobster. You know it's true. He did that to her. Made her pregnant. She couldn't bear it."

"You're wrong, Frank," Molly said.

Susannah began to cry, a few little yelps, then a steady wail. Jesse swore, knowing Amanda too well. He put his shoulder against the door, praying he could time it right.

AMANDA HEARD her baby cry, a primal call that reverberated through her body. She'd already tried the back door. It was locked. She'd moved to one of the windows and found she couldn't get it unstuck. Now, she hurried to another window. It was partially open. She shoved it up enough that she could squeeze through.

She dropped into a large clawfoot bathtub and stood for a moment, listening. Susannah's cries clutched at her heart. She could hear voices. A man's. And Molly's.

"I saw the heart, Frank," Molly was saying. "He had that heart Roxie always wore."

"Got it from that damned mobster," Frank said,

sounding angry. "That J. B. Crowe. Humanitarian, like hell."

"No, Frank," Molly said. "It wasn't him. I never told you because you didn't like any of the boys that came 'round, but it wasn't that one. It was the other boy. Billy. Billy Kincaid. I saw her with him once."

"Don't do this to me, woman," Frank warned.

"Oh, Frank, how could you have left Roxie's baby beside some road in a box? How could you have lied to me all these years? How could you have done something like this? Why now, Frank? Why now?"

"This isn't the first time, Molly," Frank said. "You think I would wait this long to get back at that monster? I almost got the other baby twenty-five years ago."

Amanda couldn't stand it any longer. She jerked open the bathroom door, praying that she could distract Frank Pickett enough that Jesse could get to Frank.

She saw the large, graying man standing over her baby. She didn't notice the gun or the woman sitting in the corner of the room crying. She rushed to her baby and scooped Susannah up into her arms before the man could react.

JESSE PUT HIS shoulder against the front door and burst into the room just seconds after Amanda. But it was already too late.

Frank was bringing the gun up, the barrel pointed at Amanda and the baby.

"No!" Jesse cried as he tried to get to Frank before he could pull the trigger.

It all happened so quickly. Molly trying to stop Frank, throwing herself out of the chair and at him. The sound of the gunshot, Molly being thrown to the floor, the sound of her head hitting the edge of the log coffee table, then silence.

At first Jesse thought Amanda had been shot. There was blood everywhere and Amanda was on her knees beside Molly, Susannah cradled in one arm, her hand on Molly's cheek.

Jesse caught Frank with a left hook and dropped the man, twisting the gun from the kidnapper's hand before he hit the floor beside his wife. Molly was on the floor lying in a pool of blood, her eyes open, her life gone.

Jesse rushed to Amanda and Susannah, seeing at once that both were fine. He shook his head at Amanda's hopeful look. Molly was dead.

He helped Amanda to her feet. She clutched Susannah in her arms. The baby had quit crying. She cooed up at her mother, kicking her tiny legs and flailing her arms. The look on Amanda's face as she gazed down at her baby almost dropped Jesse to his knees. He looked at mother and daughter, his heart bursting. Finally, Susannah was safe in her mother's arms. At least for the moment.

"Molly?" Frank said as he laid his head on her body. "It's going to be all right, now, Molly. Everything is going to be just fine. Tomorrow I'll take you and Roxie fishing. You'd like that, wouldn't you?"

Chapter Sixteen

In the wee hours of the morning, the ambulance finally pulled away, the siren a low, mournful moan dying away in the distance.

"Frank has confessed everything," Sheriff Wilson told Jesse. "You're both free to go."

Jesse glanced to the van where Amanda lay curled in the back, her baby beside her, both having fallen into an exhausted sleep. Frank was under arrest. Molly was dead.

"Frank was never the same after Roxie killed herself," a neighboring cabin owner kept saying. "He was just never the same."

When the sheriff finally said he could go, Jesse got into the van and drove south. He called his boss on Amanda's cell phone and filled him in on everything that had happened, knowing he was going to catch hell over the decisions he had made. At one point, Jesse had held in his hands evidence against J. B. Crowe, something his boss wasn't

likely to forget. Nor was Jesse likely to forget that
his boss was the only one who had known he and
Amanda had gone to Red River. Amanda didn't
wake until he'd almost reached Dallas. With Susannah secured in the car seat she had packed in
the back, she planted a kiss on the sleeping baby's
cheek before slipping into the passenger seat next
to him.

He could tell how hard it was to let Susannah
out of her arms. What had ever made him think
she didn't love her baby? Could have abandoned
Susannah? Or pretended the infant had been kidnapped, using Susannah as Gage had?

"Where are we?" Amanda asked, glancing
around.

"Almost to Dallas."

Her eyebrow shot up.

"I can't let you leave the country," he said hurriedly. He could feel her gaze on him.

"Can't? Or won't?" she asked.

"Can't," he said as he pulled over in the shade
of a large tree alongside a city park. The sun was
coming up, big and bright. It was going to be another hot one in this part of Texas.

He cut the engine and turned in his seat. "I've
been thinking about this a lot."

"Yes?" she asked and waited.

His heart pounded with just the thought of what
he wanted to say. Words he'd never uttered to an-

other woman. But they seemed right. And yet, only a fool wouldn't realize the danger in what he was about to propose.

"Amanda," he said, taking her hand in his. "I *can't* let you go off alone with Susannah. You won't be safe. No matter where you run, either your father or Mickie Ferraro and his henchmen or someone else with a grudge against your father will be looking for you. There is only one place I can think of that you and Susannah would be safe. And that's with me."

AMANDA HELD her breath, her gaze locked to his. He wanted to come with them. Was it possible he would give up being a cop to protect her and Susannah? She could feel her heart banging in her chest. For the first time in her life, she knew exactly what she wanted. This man. A family for Susannah. A normal life. She wasn't sure what that would entail—let alone how to get one—but she had the feeling that with Jesse, anything was possible. As long as he'd go with her and Susannah.

"With you?" she managed to ask.

And the next thing she knew, she was in his arms. His mouth found hers, his kiss soft and sweet and full of promise. He kissed her deeply, passionately, as if this morning was all they had. Then he drew back and gazed into her eyes, making her melt inside.

"I love you, Amanda. I want to marry you."

His words filled her, as satisfying as any she'd ever heard. "Oh, Jesse, my love." She hugged him tightly. "Oh, yes, I knew you'd come with us. We can go to Europe. Or maybe—"

He pulled back abruptly, his eyes dark, a frown furrowing his brows. "No, Amanda."

She stared at him, uncomprehending. Hadn't he just told her he loved her? Hadn't he just asked her to marry him?

"We can't run all our lives," he said. "What kind of life would that be for Susannah? For us?"

"What are you saying?" she managed to ask.

"We stay here."

She gaped at him. "Are you mad?" Finally, she'd met the man of her dreams and he was stark raving crazy.

"It's the only way," he said grabbing her upper arms, forcing her to face him. "Listen to me. I've thought about this. I've thought about nothing else since we made love. I've been crazy for you since the first time I laid eyes on you. But these past few days, I've fallen in love with you. I can't imagine life without you."

"But Jesse—"

He put a finger to her lips. "Sweetheart, running away won't help. Your father would find us. Or Mickie. Amanda, we need your father's protection."

"Now I know you've lost your mind," she cried. "You aren't suggesting—"

"Your father loves you, Amanda. He loves his granddaughter. I think you realize now that he wouldn't harm you or Susannah. I'm not saying you can change him. Or change his past. I'm not saying eventually he won't go to prison for some of the things he's done. But I believe he will try to be a better man for the two of you and for right now, that's enough."

"He would never allow me to marry a cop," she said emphatically.

Jesse grinned. "There's only one way to find out."

"He'll kill you!" she cried.

"His future son-in-law? I don't think so. You forget, I'm Billy Kincaid's son and J.B. knows it."

She cupped his wonderfully handsome face in her hands. "Do you really believe it's possible that we could have a normal life?" Yet even as she asked the question, she knew it just might be. For that, she would do anything. Even go back to her father's.

"Well?" Jesse asked. "I promise it's only temporary."

She pulled his face to her and kissed him lightly on the mouth. "You make me believe anything is possible."

POSSIBLE OR NOT, it was the only option Jesse could come up with. They couldn't run. J.B.'s resources were too far-reaching. And as far as Jesse knew, Mickie Ferraro still hadn't given up trying to kill Amanda. J.B. could make sure that Mickie was stopped. The Crowe compound could be a temporary sanctuary. Or the lion's den, Jesse thought as he neared the gate.

Jesse didn't believe for a minute that J. B. Crowe could change. Or would want to. Not for all the love in the world. Not even for his daughter's. Or granddaughter's.

But Jesse knew if he could get J.B.'s blessing, he would be able to protect Amanda from not only the mob—but from J.B. himself. As for Mickie Ferraro, if Jesse knew J.B., the mobster would take care of Mickie once and for all.

All Jesse knew was that he and Amanda and Susannah couldn't run the rest of their lives. Nor could they ever hide from the mob. Their only hope was going inside.

He knew he was taking a hell of a chance, but he had Amanda and Susannah. And he was Billy Kincaid's son. Jesse just hoped that was enough.

J.B. had placed a new guard at the gate now, a man Jesse had seen before, a man who'd seen him as well. The guard recognized Amanda immediately. His gaze went from her to Jesse, then to the back of the van where boxes and suitcases were piled high, to the seat where Susannah, now awake, smiled and laughed as if she'd already forgotten those few days in April 2001 that she'd been lost to her mother.

Excitedly, the guard called up to the main house on a cell phone, announced who was at the gate, then held the phone away from his ear. Jesse could hear J.B. yelling from where he sat.

"Yes, Mr. Crowe," the guard said when he got the chance. The gate opened and the guard motioned them through hurriedly.

J.B. was standing outside when they drove up. Neither Death nor Destruction seemed to be around, but Jesse would bet they weren't far off.

"Remember," Jesse whispered. "He loves you." But did J.B. love her enough to accept Jesse's terms? That would be the question.

AMANDA NODDED and opened her door. She'd never seen her father scared. Nor had she ever seen him cry before. He pulled her into his arms and hugged her tightly and she hugged him back. Jesse was right. J. B. Crowe was her father. Good or bad.

Amanda felt Jesse behind her. He'd gotten Susannah out of her car seat and now held her in his arms. He was looking down at Susannah's little face and smiling in a way that made her heart purr.

Without a word, Jesse handed Crowe his granddaughter. J.B. took her, holding her awkwardly, and Amanda realized this was the first time he'd actually held Susannah. She stared at the pair, wondering just what the power of love could accomplish. Because in her father's eyes she saw his love for her. For his granddaughter.

After a moment, she took her daughter from him. "There is a lot I need to tell you," she said.

"Yes," her father agreed. He looked to Jesse.

"You know who he is, don't you?" she asked.

"So it is true," J.B. said. "You're Billy's son."

Jesse nodded. "I'm in love with your daughter. And I'm a cop."

J.B. nodded slowly. "I see. Perhaps we should step inside."

Epilogue

It was to be the biggest wedding of the year, maybe of the century. J.B. Crowe had spared no expense. The guest list was huge and as varied as any wedding in history, from mobsters to cops to the governor himself. Even Olivia flew home from New York for the affair and to help with the hurried arrangements. Few people had ever been inside the Crowe compound. Most would never see it again.

But for one day, J.B. Crowe would open the doors and let the world in to see his only daughter marry the man she loved. The story had broken on page one of the Dallas papers and quickly spread across the country. *Governor Kincaid's Cop Nephew to Marry Mobster's Daughter.*

The story about Mickie Ferraro's accidental drowning in White Lake got buried on a back page of the same day's paper, but Jesse saw it and knew Ferraro's death had been no accident. J.B., good to his word, had taken care of it. Just like he had the wedding.

Jesse had watched J.B. with his daughter and granddaughter, pleased with the mobster's acting job. J.B. had seemingly convinced Amanda that he wanted to change. That he could change. She seemed deeply touched by her father's acceptance of a cop into the family.

Jesse could tell that she also wanted to believe that J.B. really hadn't had anything to do with Diana Kincaid's disappearance. Or the black market baby ring. J.B. swore his men had been operating it independently of him and he would see that it was stopped at once.

"I want to change," J.B. had told Amanda. "You have to admit, letting a cop marry into the family is a start."

Amanda had leaned up to give her father a kiss on his cheek, her eyes full of tears.

"I just want you and Susannah to be happy," J.B. had said.

That, Jesse thought, Amanda *could* believe. But for those few days before the wedding, Amanda seemed to enjoy the closeness she and her father shared. Like a lull before a storm, Jesse thought.

One night over a glass of brandy in his study, J.B. told them about the night he went to see Roxie, the night Jesse was born. He saw Frank leaving in his car. Even thought he heard a baby cry. But he'd been too upset over Billy's death to understand what he'd seen, what it meant.

Like everyone else, J.B. had believed the baby

died at birth. That Roxie had gone into premature labor after hearing about Billy's death and because of complications, lost not only her baby, but later her will to live.

J.B. often held his granddaughter and seemed to take great pleasure in having the house full of life. Sometimes Jesse would catch him watching his daughter and granddaughter, a sadness in his gaze.

Even Eunice and Malcolm treated Jesse as if he was family. Consuela cried a lot, her happiness running over, as she made wonderful meals and raced about waiting on them as if they were royalty.

"Amanda and I will be leaving right after the wedding," Jesse reminded J.B. Amanda didn't want her baby raised behind fences and bars. She desperately wanted that normal life that Jesse had promised her. And Jesse planned on it beginning right after they were married.

J.B. had only nodded. It was obvious he didn't want to lose his daughter, but maybe part of him realized he already had.

Jesse took Amanda up to meet his parents the day after their return to the Crowe estate. Amanda took to them instantly and they her, just as he'd expected.

"You made a huge hit with my folks," Jesse told her on the way home.

"They are wonderful."

"They sure loved you and Susannah. As soon

as we get married, they'll be expecting us to have more children. What do you think?''

She'd smiled. ''I think we should start working on it soon. I've always liked the idea of a lot of kids, close in age. I can't believe I've finally gotten the large family I've always dreamed of. Your brothers and sisters are great.''

He'd laughed. ''We'll see how great you think they are when you see them every holiday and every birthday and every—''

She interrupted him with a kiss. ''I can't wait.''

''Soon,'' he'd promised and he'd seen something in her gaze.... She knew, he thought. She knew he'd made a deal with her father.

And he knew that when J.B. went back to business as usual, Amanda would wash her hands of her father once and for all. And maybe, like him, she knew it was just a matter of time.

But she never said anything. Nor he.

He'd had a long talk with his parents about what he'd found out in Red River. They had never known who his real parents were but had always feared they might be people who would come after Jesse some day.

He loved Marie and Pete McCall even more now, knowing that they had adopted him, knowing what they had gone through all those years, worrying about the biological parents possibly showing up one day.

He and Amanda had also visited the governor

and his wife a few times in Austin. Jesse told him about Brice and the other cops who'd come after them that night, unsure just who the cops worked for, and Jesse's suspicions about his boss. Kincaid had promised to look into it. He'd also offered Jesse a job on a special government task force, making it clear that he still planned to shut down organized crime in Texas.

While he'd heard from his daughter Diana and she was safe and swore she hadn't been kidnapped by J. B. Crowe, Kincaid wasn't sure if he could make the wedding or not. Jesse understood.

ON THE BIG DAY, when all the wedding preparations had been made and the Crowe compound had changed more dramatically than even J. B. Crowe himself had appeared to, J.B. called Jesse down to his study.

"I want you to have this," J.B. said, handing Jesse the heart and chain that Billy Kincaid had worn until his death.

Jesse put the two odd shaped hearts together for the first time. They formed a perfect small heart of solid gold. "Thank you, J.B. I can't tell you how much this means to me."

The older man had nodded awkwardly. "Promise me you'll look after my girls."

"I promise," Jesse said.

Outside music played on the large lawn and a crowd began to gather. Dressed in his tuxedo, Jesse went down to stand at the altar with his two brothers as attendants, and wait for his bride. He held the heart in his pocket, balled in his palm, a reminder of the past—and his hopes for the future.

Then he saw Amanda coming behind the long line of bridesmaids, three of them his sisters. She took his breath away.

His beautiful bride appeared at the end of the long runway with J.B. by her side. Jesse wanted to remember J.B. this way, he thought. A father escorting his only daughter down the aisle.

When they reached Jesse, J.B. handed Amanda to him, a warning look in his eye.

"Make my daughter happy," J.B. whispered.

"I'm sure going to try."

When the preacher finally pronounced them man and wife, Jesse lifted Amanda's veil and kissed his bride, then he pulled the heart and gold chain from his pocket and held it out to her. Tears welled in her eyes as she slipped it over her head, the two hearts finally united.

"Forever," he said, against all odds. And as he and Amanda walked down the aisle, he had the strangest feeling that Billy and Roxie were watching. And that they heartily approved.

Don't miss

UNCONDITIONAL SURRENDER

by Joanna Wayne,
available next month
from Harlequin Intrigue.

Chapter One

Pain ripped through Diana Kincaid's body with a force that seemed to split her in half. She clutched the top rail of the bed and willed her body to prevail.

Breathe and push. Breathe and push.

"She doesn't look too good, Doc."

The voice was male, brusque, tinged with a hardness that seared into her mind as the next round of contractions hit. She knew it was the taller of her two kidnappers who was talking, the one built like a heavyweight wrestler. His head was shaved and a half dozen tattoos decorated his burly arms. He went by only one name. Conan.

"Can't you do something to hurry this process along?" Conan moved in closer to the bed, and the odor of his cologne gagged her. She coughed and gasped for air as her stomach turned itself inside out.

"She's doing just fine on her own. I can feel the head now. A few more good pushes and we'll have the baby."

The baby. Her baby. Fighting its way into this living hell even though it wasn't due for another two weeks. The trauma of the kidnapping had overloaded Diana's system, initiated labor before her time.

She pushed hard and tried unsuccessfully to bite back a scream. "Alex. Alex! Please help me." Her cry filled the room, bounced off the walls, reverberated against the darkness that swirled through her mind.

It wasn't supposed to be like this. She should be in a hospital, should have a real doctor and nurses. And her parents should be standing beside her, holding her hands, reassuring her. She should be anywhere but stuck in this terrifying existence.

She closed her eyes, bit her bottom lip and forced the images from her mind. None of it mattered now. Nothing mattered except that her baby was born safe and healthy.

Her baby. Alex's baby, even though he was no longer alive to know it. "Alllllex?" The scream felt as if it were shredding the lining from her dry throat.

"He can't help you," the man called Doc urged. "Just push. Push for all you're worth. This is it."

A back-breaking contraction washed over her and this time she could feel the baby moving, feel new life through the crush of pain.

"Here it comes." The man's voice rose in anticipation. "The head is almost out."

"Damn ugly creature," Conan exclaimed. "It's all bloody."

"Bloody." Her head swam and her heart seemed to crack and shoot shivers of itself against the wall of her chest. "Please. Tell me my baby's all right."

"Baby's fine. All systems go."

"And look at that," Conan said. "It's a girl. Just what we need."

A daughter. She had her name all picked out. Alexandra, for the father she'd never know. Somehow, she had to believe he was watching over them, protecting them even through this unending nightmare.

Diana strained to hear the cries of her newborn daughter, thankful that Alexandra's wails drowned out the voices of the two monsters who'd presided over the birth. "Let me see her," she pleaded. "Let me hold her."

"Give me a minute to get her cleaned up and she's all yours."

Conan leaned over her. "Just don't get too attached. She won't be yours for long."

"What do you mean?"

"Cut the woman some slack," Doc said. "She's been through a lot."

"Yeah? You worried about the rich bitch? I thought you doctors were supposed to be immune to other people's suffering. But, that's right, you're not a doctor, are you? Just some miserable louse who couldn't cut it."

"I could have. I just got sidetracked."

"I think *addicted* is the word you're looking for."

Diana shut out the taunting, biting insults of the two men. She was so tired. But it was over. At least the birth was. She longed to just close her eyes and rest, but she didn't dare. She had to find a way to escape with her baby.

"Do you still want to hold her?" Doc asked.

"Yes, please."

"She's a big one. Never know she came early. And her lungs are definitely working."

She opened her arms, and he placed the baby inside them. She fit perfectly, so tiny, so precious. Her features swam in the moisture that glazed Diana's eyes. Not bothering to fight the tears, she let them flow as she touched each perfect finger, each perfect toe.

"You're beautiful," she crooned. "You have your dad's eyes."

"Could be, but she's got your hair. Red as the inside of a summer watermelon." Doc smiled from across the room, as if they were friends and he and the brute called Conan hadn't kidnapped her and brought her to this terrible rundown cabin.

She tried to ignore him, to pretend neither of them were there. She needed to share this moment with her daughter, their first bonding outside the womb. It would only happen once and the memory would have to last a lifetime. Rolling onto her side, she trailed her fingers down every inch of her precious baby, memorizing the shape of her face, the color of her hair and eyes, the curve of her mouth.

"Your dad would have loved you very much, Alexandra, but he can't be with us. So I'll love you enough for the both of us. I'll be here for you—always."

"Isn't that special. Makes you want to cry, doesn't it, Doc?"

Conan's voice broke into her thoughts, spoiling the beauty of the moment. But she couldn't let them rob her of this. Holding Alexandra, feeling her heartbeat and watching her breathe. Those were the only things that made sense.

She touched her lips to the top of her baby's head. "I love you so much," she whispered. "I'll take care of you and keep you safe. No matter what, I'll keep you safe.''

And she would. Somehow.

Or die trying.

Harlequin truly does make any time special....
This year we are celebrating weddings in style!

To help us celebrate, we want you to tell us how wearing the Harlequin wedding gown will make your wedding day special. As the grand prize, Harlequin will offer one lucky bride the chance to **"Walk Down the Aisle" in the Harlequin wedding gown!**

There's more...

For her honeymoon, she and her groom will spend five nights at the **Hyatt Regency Maui.** As part of this five-night honeymoon at the hotel renowned for its romantic attractions, the couple will enjoy a candlelit dinner for two in Swan Court, a sunset sail on the hotel's catamaran, and duet spa treatments.

To enter, please write, in, 250 words or less, how wearing the Harlequin wedding gown will make your wedding day special. The entry will be judged based on its emotionally compelling nature, its originality and creativity, and its sincerity. This contest is open to Canadian and U.S. residents only and to those who are 18 years of age and older. There is no purchase necessary to enter. Void where prohibited. See further contest rules attached. Please send your entry to:

Walk Down the Aisle Contest

In Canada	In U.S.A.
P.O. Box 637	P.O. Box 9076
Fort Erie, Ontario	3010 Walden Ave.
L2A 5X3	Buffalo, NY 14269-9076

You can also enter by visiting www.eHarlequin.com
Win the Harlequin wedding gown and the vacation of a lifetime!
The deadline for entries is October 1, 2001.

PHWDACONT1

HARLEQUIN WALK DOWN THE AISLE TO MAUI CONTEST 1197
OFFICIAL RULES
NO PURCHASE NECESSARY TO ENTER

1. To enter, follow directions published in the offer to which you are responding. Contest begins April 2, 2001, and ends on October 1, 2001. Method of entry may vary. Mailed entries must be postmarked by October 1, 2001, and received by October 8, 2001.

2. Contest entry may be, at times, presented via the Internet, but will be restricted solely to residents of certain geographic areas that are disclosed on the Web site. To enter via the Internet, if permissible, access the Harlequin Web site (www.eHarlequin.com) and follow the directions displayed online. Online entries must be received by 11:59 p.m. E.S.T. on October 1, 2001.

   In lieu of submitting an entry online, enter by mail by hand-printing (or typing) on an 8½" x 11" plain piece of paper, your name, address (including zip code), Contest number/name and in 250 words or fewer, why winning a Harlequin wedding dress would make your wedding day special. Mail via first-class mail to: Harlequin Walk Down the Aisle Contest 1197, (in the U.S.) P.O. Box 9076, 3010 Walden Avenue, Buffalo, NY 14269-9076, (in Canada) P.O. Box 637, Fort Erie, Ontario L2A 5X3, Canada.

   Limit one entry per person, household address and e-mail address. Online and/or mailed entries received from persons residing in geographic areas in which Internet entry is not permissible will be disqualified.

3. Contests will be judged by a panel of members of the Harlequin editorial, marketing and public relations staff based on the following criteria:

   - Originality and Creativity—50%
   - Emotionally Compelling—25%
   - Sincerity—25%

   In the event of a tie, duplicate prizes will be awarded. Decisions of the judges are final.

4. All entries become the property of Torstar Corp. and will not be returned. No responsibility is assumed for lost, late, illegible, incomplete, inaccurate, nondelivered or misdirected mail or misdirected e-mail, for technical, hardware or software failures of any kind, lost or unavailable network connections, or failed, incomplete, garbled or delayed computer transmission or any human error which may occur in the receipt or processing of the entries in this Contest.

5. Contest open only to residents of the U.S. (except Puerto Rico) and Canada, who are 18 years of age or older, and is void wherever prohibited by law; all applicable laws and regulations apply. Any litigation within the Province of Quebec respecting the conduct or organization of a publicity contest may be submitted to the Régie des alcools, des courses et des jeux for a ruling. Any litigation respecting the awarding of a prize may be submitted to the Régie des alcools, des courses et des jeux only for the purpose of helping the parties reach a settlement. Employees and immediate family members of Torstar Corp. and D. L. Blair, Inc., their affiliates, subsidiaries and all other agencies, entities and persons connected with the use, marketing or conduct of this Contest are not eligible to enter. Taxes on prizes are the sole responsibility of winners. Acceptance of any prize offered constitutes permission to use winner's name, photograph or other likeness for the purposes of advertising, trade and promotion on behalf of Torstar Corp., its affiliates and subsidiaries without further compensation to the winner, unless prohibited by law.

6. Winners will be determined no later than November 15, 2001, and will be notified by mail. Winners will be required to sign and return an Affidavit of Eligibility within 15 days after winner notification. Noncompliance within that time period may result in disqualification and an alternative winner may be selected. Winners of trip must execute a Release of Liability prior to ticketing and must possess required travel documents (e.g. passport, photo ID) where applicable. Trip must be completed by November 2002. No substitution of prize permitted by winner. Torstar Corp. and D. L. Blair, Inc., their parents, affiliates, and subsidiaries are not responsible for errors in printing or electronic presentation of Contest, entries and/or game pieces. In the event of printing or other errors which may result in unintended prize values or duplication of prizes, all affected game pieces or entries shall be null and void. If for any reason the Internet portion of the Contest is not capable of running as planned, including infection by computer virus, bugs, tampering, unauthorized intervention, fraud, technical failures, or any other causes beyond the control of Torstar Corp. which corrupt or affect the administration, secrecy, fairness, integrity or proper conduct of the Contest, Torstar Corp. reserves the right, at its sole discretion, to disqualify any individual who tampers with the entry process and to cancel, terminate, modify or suspend the Contest or the Internet portion thereof. In the event of a dispute regarding an online entry, the entry will be deemed submitted by the authorized holder of the e-mail account submitted at the time of entry. Authorized account holder is defined as the natural person who is assigned to an e-mail address by an Internet access provider, online service provider or other organization that is responsible for arranging e-mail address for the domain associated with the submitted e-mail address. **Purchase or acceptance of a product offer does not improve your chances of winning.**

7. Prizes: (1) Grand Prize—A Harlequin wedding dress (approximate retail value: $3,500) and a 5-night/6-day honeymoon trip to Maui, HI, including round-trip air transportation provided by Maui Visitors Bureau from Los Angeles International Airport (winner is responsible for transportation to and from Los Angeles International Airport) and a Harlequin Romance Package, including hotel accomodations (double occupancy) at the Hyatt Regency Maui Resort and Spa, dinner for (2) two at Swan Court, a sunset sail on Kiele V and a spa treatment for the winner (approximate retail value: $4,000); (5) Five runner-up prizes of a $1000 gift certificate to selected retail outlets to be determined by Sponsor (retail value $1000 ea.). Prizes consist of only those items listed as part of the prize. Limit one prize per person. All prizes are valued in U.S. currency.

8. For a list of winners (available after December 17, 2001) send a self-addressed, stamped envelope to: Harlequin Walk Down the Aisle Contest 1197 Winners, P.O. Box 4200 Blair, NE 68009-4200 or you may access the www.eHarlequin.com Web site through January 15, 2002.

Contest sponsored by Torstar Corp., P.O. Box 9042, Buffalo, NY 14269-9042, U.S.A.

PHWDACONT2

Where the bond of family, tradition and honor run as deep and are as vast as the great Lone Star state, that's...

Texas families are at the heart of the next Harlequin 12-book continuity series.

HARLEQUIN®

INTRIGUE

is proud to launch this brand-new series of books by some of your very favorite authors.

Look for

SOMEONE S BABY
by Dani Sinclair
On sale May 2001

SECRET BODYGUARD
by B.J. Daniels
On sale June 2001

UNCONDITIONAL SURRENDER
by Joanna Wayne
On sale July 2001

Available at your favorite retail outlet.

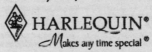

HARLEQUIN®
Makes any time special ®

Visit us at www.eHarlequin.com

HITT

BECAUSE TROUBLE SOMETIMES COMES IN TWOS...

HARLEQUIN®
INTRIGUE®

Delivers *two* times the romance
and *two* times the suspense
from *two* of your favorite authors in

DOUBLE EXPOSURE

THE MYSTERIOUS TWIN
by Leona Karr
July 2001

HIS ONLY DESIRE
by Adrianne Lee
August 2001

THIS SUMMER IS BOUND TO BE *TWICE* AS HOT!

Available at your favorite retail outlet.

HARLEQUIN®
Makes any time special ®

Visit us at www.eHarlequin.com

HIDEXP